It's a battle betw

The life of the king of the island kingdom of Zaki hangs in the balance after a major cardiac event leaves him needing life-saving surgery.

Neither of his two sons, princes Raed and Amir, are ready to return home to step into their father's shoes. Raed because he has the career he has always dreamed of as a neurosurgeon in London, and Amir because he and daughter, Farah, are still recovering from the terrible accident that claimed the life of his wife.

But when duty calls, the sons must answer.

And love? Well, love always finds a way…

Fall in love with Raed and Soraya in
Surgeon Prince's Fake Fiancée

Discover what awaits Amir and Isolde in
A Mother for His Little Princess

Both available now!

Dear Reader,

Prince Amir is ready to step up when his older brother walks away from his position in the royal family. Although he has a life in London, a family and a surgical career, he's always done the right thing. Sometimes to his detriment. Including staying too long in a loveless marriage. His plans to go back to his home country are put on hold when his wife is killed and his daughter seriously injured in a car crash.

He channels everything into helping his daughter, Farah, walk again and the only person he has to turn to is Isolde, the physiotherapist helping Farah. Fun and supportive, she's everything he and his daughter need to move past their grief.

When his older brother, Raed, and Isolde's sister, Soraya, get married, they travel out to the island of Zaki together. Away from the hospital setting, those feelings of companionship develop into something more. But a family commitment was never in free-spirited Isolde's plans.

Will a fling at the wedding prove to be enough?

Not likely!

Hopefully you'll enjoy the drama and glamour as the pair travel to the royal palace for the wedding of the year!

Love,

Karin xx

A MOTHER FOR HIS
LITTLE PRINCESS

KARIN BAINE

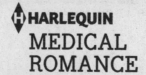

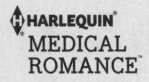

HARLEQUIN®
MEDICAL
ROMANCE™

Recycling programs
for this product may
not exist in your area.

ISBN-13: 978-1-335-59519-5

A Mother for His Little Princess

Copyright © 2023 by Karin Baine

For questions and comments about the quality of this book, please contact us at CustomerService@Harlequin.com.

Harlequin Enterprises ULC
22 Adelaide St. West, 41st Floor
Toronto, Ontario M5H 4E3, Canada
www.Harlequin.com

Printed in U.S.A.

Karin Baine lives in Northern Ireland with her husband, two sons and her out-of-control notebook collection. Her mother and her grandmother's vast collection of books inspired her love of reading and her dream of becoming a Harlequin author. Now she can tell people she has a *proper* job! You can follow Karin on Twitter @karinbaine1 or visit her website for the latest news, karinbaine.com.

Books by Karin Baine

Harlequin Medical Romance

Carey Cove Midwives
Festive Fling to Forever

Royal Docs
Surgeon Prince's Fake Fiancée

One Night with Her Italian Doc
The Surgeon and the Princess
The Nurse's Christmas Hero
Wed for Their One Night Baby
A GP to Steal His Heart
Single Dad for the Heart Doctor
Falling Again for the Surgeon
Nurse's Risk with the Rebel

Harlequin Romance

Pregnant Princess at the Altar

Visit the Author Profile page
at Harlequin.com for more titles.

For Charlotte, who helped me achieve so much xx

**Praise for
Karin Baine**

"Emotionally enchanting! The story was fast-paced, emotionally charged and oh so satisfying!"
—*Goodreads* on *Their One-Night Twin Surprise*

CHAPTER ONE

'I THOUGHT I was the princess in the family,' Isolde Yarrow teased her sister over their video call.

She'd taken the opportunity between her physiotherapy patients to phone Soraya and see how the wedding preparations were going. In just a few weeks Soraya was going to be marrying Raed Ayad, Crown Prince of Zaki, an island in the Persian Gulf, to become royalty herself.

It was a long way from the life they'd had growing up when Soraya had worked hard to put food on the table for them both after their parents died, and Isolde was thrilled that her big sis finally had someone to look out for her for a change. Though it didn't mean she wasn't missing her now that she'd moved halfway across the world to take up her new role in the royal family.

'You will always be my little princess, Isolde, though I'm not sure it's a role I'll ever get used to.' Soraya sighed but Isolde could hear the happiness in her voice.

'I'm sure you'll get used to a life of luxury and people waiting on you hand and foot,' she joked, though her sister deserved every second of it after the sacrifices she'd made for her over the years.

'I admit, there are plenty of perks, but we're certainly not letting the grass grow under our feet. We mightn't be able to work in the health service any more, but we're still trying to make a difference. I can't wait until you come over and see all of the charity projects we're working on.'

It was a complete change of lifestyle for her sister, moving abroad to marry a prince, and leaving her career as a cardiac surgeon behind, but Isolde knew she wouldn't have done it unless she loved Raed very much. Something that was entirely reciprocated. Isolde had seen for herself how quickly they'd fallen in love, even though it was supposed to have been a fake romance to divert attention away from the King's ill health at the time.

Raed was a vast improvement on Soraya's ex-husband, Frank, who had taken advantage of her kind nature, cheating on her and running up huge debt, which had led to her sleeping in Isolde's spare room for months after the divorce. Isolde too had been going through a break-up at the time, which had left her sceptical about the whole idea of romance. But Soraya and Raed were now making her question that vow she'd made not to get involved with another man again, given how happy they were together. Though she doubted she'd dip her toes into the commitment pool ever again.

When Isolde was just ten years old, Soraya eighteen, their father had died of lung cancer. Followed less than a year later by their mother. Years of heavy smoking and working in smoky clubs had taken its toll and left Soraya to take care of everything and everyone. Seeing the burden of responsibility left upon her sibling's shoulders, Isolde had decided life was for living. She wasn't going to get tied down with no life to call her own. Instead she'd drifted from one job to another, sofa-surfed, and made sure never to get bogged down in a serious relationship. Then Olly had come into her life and she'd lost all sense when it came to her heart, and the very definition of who she was.

She'd fallen hard for the earnest school-teacher. He'd convinced her to get some qualifications so she had a better career path than waitressing and bartending, and she'd trained as a physiotherapist and got a full time position at the London Central Hospital, where she'd been working for the last three years. The same hospital Soraya had transferred to when her marriage had fallen apart and she'd wanted a new start.

Isolde's life with Olly had been comfortable, but he'd had to go and spoil it all by talking about the future. Marriage hadn't seemed like a huge step forward when they'd already been living together for so long, but the family bombshell had proved too much for their relationship. Too much of an ask for Isolde.

He'd wanted children, expected her to put her new career on hold to have babies. It had seemed to her in that moment that she was the one being expected to make all the compromises in the relationship, and having a family she didn't want wasn't going to be good for anyone. Not least the innocent lives Olly wanted to bring into the world. She'd seen the toll it had taken on Soraya raising a family she hadn't been fully prepared for and didn't want that life for herself.

In the end neither she nor Olly had wanted to back down, and, with very different ideas of how their future should be, they'd parted ways. Isolde hadn't had the heart to even date since, but she was pleased that Soraya had seemingly found her happy ever after with a handsome prince. Although if she was allowed to have a selfish moan about the situation it would be that she'd been left on her own since her housemate had moved out. She should be enjoying having her own space again, but this was the first time in her life she didn't have her sister around to support her. It was going to take some getting used to.

'I'm counting the days, sis.' Literally. Isolde had been crossing off the days until the wedding on her calendar until she could see her sister again.

'Amir and Farah will be coming too. Oh, it seems so long since we saw everyone. I'm as excited about your visit as the wedding.' Soraya laughed, and Isolde's heart ached a little more. She longed to be with her having fun and putting the world to rights over cocktails and dinner, but she couldn't tell her and put a dampener on her mood. It was about time Soraya had some happiness for herself and Isolde wouldn't do anything to spoil that for her.

'I'm just about to catch up with him. I've got an appointment with one of his patients.' Amir, Raed's younger brother, was a thoracic surgeon in the hospital so their paths crossed often. More so this last year since she'd started treating his daughter, nine-year-old Farah, who'd suffered a spinal injury in the car crash that had also taken her mother away from her.

Now Amir and Isolde's siblings were getting married, and they had no other family here in England with them, they'd been seeing a lot of one another. In a strictly professional capacity only, of course.

'Say hello from us, and we'll see you all soon.' Soraya blew a kiss and waved goodbye.

'Love you, sis.' Isolde swallowed down the lump in her throat before she made a fool of herself in the middle of the rehab unit, or, worse, upset any of her patients by bursting into tears. Instead she plastered on a smile and gave a thumbs up pretending she didn't feel completely lost without her big sister who had always been there, protecting her, and supporting her financially and emotionally over the years. It was time she grew up and stood on her own two feet and there was nothing to be gained from upsetting Soraya when she was enjoying her new life.

Isolde took a deep breath and tried to compose herself, only for the feel of someone's hand on her back to make her jump.

'What the hell——?' She turned around sharply to see who had invaded her personal space and found tall, dark and handsome Amir standing there with his hands in the air as though waiting for the firing squad to take aim.

'Sorry. I didn't mean to startle you. I've been calling out to you the whole way since I saw you walk through Reception, but I think you were on the phone.'

'Yeah, I was talking to Soraya, sorry. She said to say hi, by the way.' Isolde offered him a smile, and though Amir smiled back, she recognised the pain behind it. 'Have you spoken to Raed?'

Amir shook his head. 'Not recently. I know he's busy with the wedding.'

Not so long ago Raed had rebelled against the idea of returning to Zaki to take up his rightful position as heir to the throne. He'd been ready to step aside in favour of Amir taking over but circumstances had changed everything. The car accident and their father's heart problems some months later had meant Raed had to be the face of the monarchy so the country didn't fall apart in the King's absence. Taken ill while visiting in London, their father had had to have his heart bypass and post-op rehab there before he was fit enough to return home. Soraya had been Raed's fake fiancée, giving the media a cover story to detract from what was really going on with the family. Except they'd fallen for each other and started a new life in Zaki in their royal roles.

It seemed Raed and Soraya had moved on quickly from the lives they'd had back in England for better things, but it wasn't so easy for those of them left behind who didn't have royal roles and a luxurious lifestyle to fill the void of missing family members. Amir's parents had returned home once his father had recovered from his heart bypass, so he no longer had anyone supporting him here in the midst of his grief and Farah's struggle to walk again.

Her incomplete spinal injury had caused some paralysis through her body and, though she had recovered movement in her upper body and no longer had breathing difficulties, she couldn't walk. She'd had surgery to reduce muscle inflammation and swelling, and muscle control came and went in her lower limbs, but her mobility remained limited.

It had been over a year now since Amir had lost his wife and Farah's mother. Isolde knew something about that kind of loss. Except she'd had Soraya to pick up the pieces and put her back together again. Amir's family were at a distance, no longer part of his daily existence and she knew how difficult that was when she'd relied on Soraya her entire life. It was like another bereavement of sorts, mourning that tangible support and having to move on without it.

'Soraya said they've been setting up all sorts of charity initiatives too. No doubt we'll find out all about it when we're over for the wedding. I'm sure Farah is excited about being a bridesmaid.' Isolde was trying to put a positive spin on it all, regardless of feeling as heartbroken as Amir looked.

'She's more worried than anything. It's going to put a spotlight on her, and with being in the wheelchair…she's not looking forward to all of the attention. I know Raed and Soraya have fostered a good relationship with the media because of the charity work and public engagements they're carrying out, but I'm not sure I want to be part of that with Farah the way she is.' It was apparent in the set of Amir's jaw and the frown furrowing his forehead that it was weighing heavily on his mind too. No doubt he was caught between doing what was right for his daughter and his family.

'I understand your concerns. She'll have all of us to look after her though, and if she wants we can put some extra time in together on her exercises, or go dress shopping, or bling out her wheelchair. Whatever would make her more comfortable on the day.' Isolde was sure that in all of the excitement Soraya and Raed had overlooked the fact his niece might be wary of her very public appearance when she was still struggling to come to terms with her life-changing injuries. She would talk to Soraya later and convey any concerns Amir and Farah had about the event and her place in the wedding party. At least she'd managed to make him smile with the idea of pimping out Farah's ride for the big day.

'She'd probably like that.'

It was nice to see Amir relax a little. He

was always so tense, concerned with every-one else's welfare. If it wasn't his daugh-ter he was fretting over, it was his patients. Although he'd been through a lot in recent times, Isolde wondered if he ever let loose once in a while.

'I'm going to work on some strengthening exercises with your pneumonia patient now, but I'll call in on Farah later if you're about?'

'Mr Douglas? I'm heading that way myself. I just wanted to check on his chest drain, if you don't mind me crashing in on your physio session?'

'Not at all. It'll be good to have you on hand in case he needs any extra pain relief.'

'Why, are you planning on torturing him today?' Amir asked with a twinkle of mis-chief glinting in his chocolate-brown eyes.

'No, I did that yesterday,' Isolde answered with just as much sass. 'However, I will be pushing him to get as mobile as possible to fast-track his recovery so we need to make sure his analgesia is adequate to compensate for the effort.'

In low-risk patients who hadn't encoun-tered any complications it was necessary to mobilise them after thoracic surgery, not only to strengthen the limbs, but to prevent any circulatory problems from occurring. Mr Douglas, who'd been admitted for surgery after pneumonia had caused a build-up of fluid on the lungs and breathing difficulties, should only need three or four days of physiotherapy before he was able to return home. If he followed Isolde's instruction.

'I will be on hand if he needs anything extra and I'll check his heart rate and blood pressure before he undertakes any exercise.'

Isolde knew with post-operative patients it was necessary to keep an eye on them at all stages of their sessions when complications could arise at any second and she was glad Amir took such a keen interest in his patients' welfare.

Just before they approached the man's bedside Amir touched her arm and said, 'I know how important physiotherapy is to my patients' recovery. Thank you for everything you do.'

And just like that, he walked away, leaving Isolde speechless. There were few surgeons who took time to acknowledge her part in the team that worked with the patients long after the surgery was over. She counted herself lucky to work with someone so generous, as well as skilled. All of his patients only ever had good things to say about him, checking in with them as he did until they were discharged from the hospital. It was just a shame such a good man had had truly awful things happen to him in his personal life.

'Mr Douglas, how are we today?' Amir asked, checking the chart hanging on the end of the bed.

'Good, Doctor. A little sore.'

'That's to be expected but I can increase the pain relief if you're too uncomfortable. Ms Yarrow is here for your physiotherapy session but I thought I'd check in on you too.' Amir stood aside to let Isolde do her job and she appreciated that he deferred to her so easily. Ego was not a problem around him, even though as a successful surgeon, and a prince, he would have every right to act superior.

'Hello, Mr Douglas. We're just going to move you into the chair to do a few exercises to start off with today. If you're in any pain at all let us know. Mr Ayad, could you help me move Mr Douglas off the bed?' Although she was capable of transferring patients herself, it would be churlish not to take advantage of an extra pair of hands where she could. Like Amir, she wasn't too proud to ask for help, or appreciate it when it was given.

'Of course.' He came around to the side of the bed and helped to position the patient so his feet were hanging over the edge.

Thoracic surgery was known to be painful and in this instance Amir would have had to go through the chest to evacuate the infection, leaving chest tubes in place to drain the fluid collected around the lungs. She had to be careful when assisting Mr Douglas out of bed to support the incision and drain sites with firm but gentle pressure, avoiding direct pressure on the areas. With one hand on the front of his chest, the other at the back, and her forearms stabilising the entire chest as much as possible, she worked with Amir to move him over onto the chair.

'Okay?' she asked the patient, while nodding her thanks to Amir for his assistance.

'Yes,' Mr Douglas confirmed, a little breathless, like herself.

'We're just going to take five minutes to do a few exercises to minimise any circulatory problems and prevent any restrictions in your chest. With your hands behind your neck I want you to move your head back, slowly extending your spine and using the back of the chair for support.' She sat on the edge of the bed and demonstrated the movement.

Mr Douglas slowly copied the action without too much trouble.

'Good. I need you to do that five times.'

She watched him carefully as he repeated the motion.

'That's it. Now if you can fold your arms across your chest and turn slowly as if you're looking one way, then another, that would be great. We'll repeat that five times too. And then if you can put your hands behind your neck again for me, we're going to bend the trunk carefully from side to side.' She watched as the man followed her instructions wincing every now and then but generally without complaint.

Amir sat quietly to one side observing as she followed with a few leg and arm exercises and she knew if there was any discomfort he would've jumped in to offer his assistance. Although it was a tad intimidating to have the surgeon watching her work, it was also reassuring that he had an interest in her work and was there should she need him. Thankfully, other than helping get Mr Douglas get back into bed again, she didn't.

'You get some sleep now. I think you deserve it,' Amir counselled as they prepared to leave.

'I'll be back again tomorrow and we'll see about getting you on your feet for a little walk about.' Isolde knew this was only the beginning of his recovery and wanted him to be prepared.

'No rest for the wicked,' Mr Douglas joshed as he laid his head back on the pillow. He was snoring before Isolde and Amir had even left the ward.

'How on earth do you manage moving these patients on your own?' Amir queried as they walked out into the corridor.

'With these.' Isolde flexed her biceps, drawing a rarely heard laugh from the surgeon. 'And a lot of patience.'

'It's a more physically demanding job than I realised.'

'Sometimes. It just depends on the patient and the circumstances. I have a good mix. I'm off now to work with a young amputee who is very feisty and independent. I'll probably have my work cut out trying to get him to let me help with anything.'

'You work very hard. I'm finished for the day but why don't you come by the house later? Maybe we can get some takeaway. I know Farah would enjoy the company. I think evenings with her dad in front of the television have lost the novelty appeal and she doesn't have many friends who want to come over much any more. I think they're having trouble adjusting to her new circumstances too.'

'That's awful. I'd love to come over and see her, but don't you think that's blurring the lines a little bit? I mean, we're colleagues, Farah's my patient…' Isolde knew there was nothing more in the invitation than providing his daughter with some female company to lift her spirits, with some dinner thrown in, but she didn't want either of them to get into trouble at work.

Amir screwed up his nose. 'We're going to be family soon anyway. I think lines have been blurred for a long time. Officially you probably won't be treating Farah much longer, and I won't tell anyone if you won't. But, if you'd rather not I understand.'

'It's fine. We'll work something out. I'm not one for rules anyway. I'll see you at eight. Text me your address,' she shouted behind her as she made her way onto the ward.

He was right, theirs was a complicated situation now because of their siblings' relationship, but Isolde didn't see the harm in spending time with Amir and Farah on a personal level. They were going to be family soon enough and neither she nor Amir were likely to confuse a takeaway at his house for anything romantic.

Amir believed Isolde when she said they would work something out. They had to. Farah was his world and he would give anything to make her happy again. It was his fault she'd lost her mother, and that she was confined to a wheelchair, so the least he could do was find a way to make her comfortable.

He was happy that his brother and Soraya had found love and were getting married, though it hadn't worked out so well for him. After spending a lifetime growing up in his brother's shadow, trying to prove that he was worthy of his position in the family to his parents too, Amir had done his best to be the perfect son. He'd studied hard, carved out a successful career, and when Raed had decided he no longer wanted to be next in line to the throne, he'd been ready to step up, willing to take on that responsibility.

Even his marriage had been a way to show his parents he was more than just the second son, the back-up plan for the real Crown Prince. He'd married the right woman from the right family, making them a true Zaki power couple. Shula's parents, wealthy aristocrats who had strong government connections, had encouraged the match, as had Amir's family. And, once Farah had come along, they had seemed like the perfect little family.

Except nothing he'd ever done had seemed to be good enough for his wife. It was only now that she was gone he could admit love had never been a strong factor in their marriage. A good match on paper keeping their respective families happy, perhaps, but in the end it hadn't been sufficient to sustain a long-lasting relationship. Until eventually Shula had told him she didn't love him and wanted a divorce so she was free to pursue other men in the hope of finding what Amir apparently couldn't give her. They'd rowed because he hadn't been able to face giving up on his marriage and admitting defeat to the world at not being able to make his wife happy. He'd wanted counselling, another chance to prove himself, but Shula hadn't and had left home in a frustrated rage.

That was the night she'd had the car accident and he'd been holding onto the guilt ever since. No one knew their marriage had been all but over. Everyone saw him as the grieving husband who'd lost the love of his life. Yes, it was still a great loss, but she'd hurt him, made it clear he'd lost her already that night. He was too embarrassed, too proud, too protective of his daughter to make that information public knowledge. So he'd kept the secret to himself, swallowed down the primal urge to scream every time someone offered their sympathy and added it to the burden of guilt he carried knowing he'd failed as a husband and father. If it took the rest of his life he would try his best to make it up to Farah.

If she wasn't comfortable being part of the royal wedding, it was up to him to find a way to help her, or remove her from the equation altogether if she didn't want to be involved. He didn't blame her. In today's society any difference in abilities was often picked apart in the press and social media and he wouldn't subject his daughter to that if he could help it. Especially when she was already experiencing some alienation from her young friends. It was only natural, he supposed, that with all of her appointments and time spent at the hospital she would get left behind, not being involved in the usual social activities of nine-year-old girls. However, he did hope that some day she would catch up and be that happy, fun-loving little girl he knew and loved again.

The doorbell sounded throughout the house and Amir's stomach did a half-flip. It was silly really. He knew it was Isolde and she was only here because he'd invited her, but she would be the only woman who'd set foot in the house since his wife died. The only reason he'd felt comfortable enough asking her over, apart from Farah needing her help, was the knowledge she wasn't likely to misinterpret this get-together as anything romantic. They were practically family and she was a part of their lives because of her close bond working with Farah. Today he'd seen firsthand how hard she worked and knew, now that her sister had moved away, she'd be returning to an empty house. He'd only thought to offer company to her, as well as himself.

So why was his pulse racing and a cold sweat breaking out on his top lip as though he were on a first date?

'Papa, aren't you going to open the door?' Farah appeared at his side looking up at him with a mixture of confusion and irritation. He knew she'd been looking forward to this since he'd told her they'd be having Isolde's company tonight.

Amir blinked, realising he'd been staring at the door as though he were about to walk into the lion's den, and finally moved to open it.

'Grab these quick before I drop them,' Isolde commanded, her blonde head bobbing up from behind a small stack of pizza boxes as she thrust them forward.

Amir's quick reflexes kicked into action and he managed to take hold of her burden before they toppled to the floor.

'Thanks,' she said, stumbling through the door carrying takeout bags in both hands. 'I didn't know what you liked so I got a selection. There's pizza, chicken wings and fries.'

'I thought we were just going to order in. I didn't expect you to bring dinner with you.' He'd planned on treating her, having something special delivered to the door, since she was a guest. This display of generosity was unexpected.

Isolde closed the door and paused in the hallway. 'No offence, Amir, but I imagined your idea of fast food was some raw sushi couriered over from a top-class restaurant. I'm more a greasy pepperoni kind of girl. Now, where's the kitchen?'

'Through here.' Farah's face lit up the minute she saw her friend and she quickly spun her wheelchair around so Isolde could follow her.

'I hope you like pizza, Farah. I got barbecue chicken, pepperoni and a tomato and cheese just in case.' Isolde shook off her coat one arm at a time as she walked through the house and casually hung it on the back of a chair in the kitchen, making herself at home.

'I've never tried it.' Farah's eyes were as wide as the pizza boxes that he slid onto the kitchen worktop as if she were about to discover some long-lost treasure.

Isolde fixed him with her piercing blue eyes and pursed her lips. 'Amir Ayad, how have you denied your daughter the greatest-tasting junk food for all this time?'

What could he do but smile and shrug as she unboxed the doughy delights?

As Isolde set to work plating the rest of their meal while he poured out the fizzy drinks she'd brought it occurred to him that she fitted so easily into their life she'd really been a blessing. Especially since his parents had returned home after Soraya and Raed, leaving him and Farah on their own in England. Although his father had recovered well, he was taking more of a back seat these days when it came to public engagements, with Raed and Soraya picking up the slack. He couldn't help but feel left out. Especially when he was the one who had been preparing to take over when the time came. Although he didn't need the extra pressure or stress at the minute, it seemed like another area that he'd failed in by not being able to fulfil his royal duties.

Isolde took a bite out of her pepperoni slice and smiled at him, seemingly unfazed by the barbecue sauce smeared around her mouth. There were no airs and graces with her, and Amir didn't feel as though he had to be on his best behaviour when he was around her. It was probably the most comfortable he'd ever been with another person other than Farah.

It was then Amir knew he'd made a big mistake inviting her into their home.

CHAPTER TWO

ISOLDE HOPED SHE hadn't overstepped the mark but she'd wanted to keep this a casual affair. If she was going to any other friend's house for a takeaway, picking up a pizza on the way wouldn't have been a big deal. She could never have known pizza wasn't on a list of permitted foods for Amir's little princess. Although, to be fair to him, he hadn't made it an issue. He'd even tucked in too.

Sitting at his breakfast bar tucking into pizza from takeaway boxes was a long way from the fancy afternoon tea they'd shared months ago with his mother, Raed and Soraya at a five-star hotel to discuss how they would publicly deal with the King's health. It was where they'd first introduced the idea of Soraya pretending to be Raed's fake fiancée to detract attention away from his family's extended stay in England. Thank goodness everything had worked out for them in the end and Raed hadn't taken Isolde up on her offer of playing the role of his future wife!

It had seemed like something exciting and fun to take on at first. The sort of mad-cap scheme the old Isolde would've been in-volved in before she'd been tamed. Although she hadn't really known Raed at the time, she'd worked with Amir, had been having physiotherapy sessions with Farah. She knew the family had been through a lot and had wanted to help when she and Soraya had been privy to their conversation over afternoon tea about the damage it could do to their country if the King's ill health was to become com-mon knowledge. They'd needed a distraction, at least one member of the family to return home, and that had ended up being Raed.

It certainly wouldn't have helped Amir to have been under any pressure to go home when he still had Farah to worry about. She was glad Soraya had agreed to accompany Raed and everything had worked out in the end. In hindsight, she wouldn't have wanted the commitment of being in another relation-ship, even a fake one, never mind the respon-sibility to a whole nation that her sister had taken on.

'I don't think I could eat another bite,' Amir said eventually, breaking the comfortable silence that had descended as they enjoyed their meal.

'I'm done too,' Farah announced, setting down her half-eaten slice of pizza, though she was wearing a great big tomato-sauce smile on her face.

'Well, what's the verdict?' she asked the pair who were leaning back patting their full bellies in appreciation.

'Yummy!'

'Okay as an occasional treat.' Amir countered his daughter's enthusiasm to remind them both that fast food wasn't a diet staple.

Something that Isolde needed to remember, since she'd done very little cooking for herself lately. She'd become so used to her big sister being the domestic goddess providing her with home-cooked meals it was difficult to get into the routine of making her own. Especially when she was the only one in the flat now and she'd been eating out rather than coming home to an empty place in the evenings. Although her sister had been a tad overbearing since her divorce and moving in, Isolde was missing her lately. Farah wasn't the only one who needed some company.

'And this was my treat,' she said brightly, justifying the feast they'd just enjoyed. Although, as Soraya's chief bridesmaid she didn't want to put on weight now so close to the wedding when the eyes of the world would be watching. She was beginning to understand Farah's anxiety around her appearance when they would all be under close scrutiny in the press.

'Next time, I'll cook,' Amir offered and coming here again, sharing her evening with him and Farah, was something she was already looking forward to.

'I didn't think princes had any need to do that. Don't you have an entourage to cater to your every whim?' Isolde knew he didn't employ any such team of staff or any of the other perks she imagined came with his title. Despite his being a prince, his daughter a princess, they didn't insist anyone used their titles in England. Probably so they could be afforded a relatively normal life here. However, she still enjoyed teasing him about the differences in their social classes.

He fixed her with an intense stare before rolling his brown eyes. 'You know I don't, but if you're volunteering for the position...'

Okay, so he could give as much as he got,

but that was what made being around him so easy. They had fun and she never had to worry at what point he was going to hurt her because they were friends, nothing more.

'I'm not. I'm going to have my hands full being Farah's personal wedding stylist.' Isolde turned her attention to the real reason she was here tonight.

The young girl sat up in her chair, alert at the mention of her name. 'You are?'

Isolde began collecting the empty boxes and wrappers from the kitchen worktops and Amir wrapped up the leftovers. 'Yes. I'll just clear this away so we can sit down and brainstorm.'

'No, you won't,' Amir said sternly, the sight of his dark frown stopping Isolde in her tracks. She really had crossed the line this time. Isolde was always telling her she acted without thinking and now she'd somehow managed to cause offence by turning up at Amir's house and taking over.

'Sorry, I just thought…'

'You're our guest. I wouldn't expect you to stay in my kitchen all night. There's a perfectly good sofa in the lounge you can sit on.' He broke into a grin, a telltale sign that he was getting his own back for her earlier tease.

'Thank you, Your Highness.' Isolde gave him a mock curtsey before following him and Farah into the living room.

Although the décor was very high end compared to her budget flat-pack furniture and cheap wallpaper, it still didn't look like the home of a prince. There was no ostentatious display of wealth painted in gold on the walls—the matt grey walls lined with candid family pictures made it look like any normal family's home. Especially with Farah's artwork and some hand-painted aeroplane models dotted around that she suspected Amir had constructed himself. If she'd expected diamond-encrusted thrones she'd have been disappointed in the comfortable corner sofa dominating the space, but everything was modest and tasteful. Just like Amir.

She waited until everyone got comfortable, including herself, as she kicked off her shoes and tucked her legs beneath her on the sofa. As if to say he was fine with her making herself at home, Amir followed suit.

'So what is it we're doing, Isolde?' Unable to contain her excitement and curiosity any longer, Farah wheeled herself across the room and positioned her chair directly in front of Isolde.

'Well, I've had a talk with Soraya. I know we've both had some dress fittings for the wedding and it hasn't been easy co-ordinating everything with her when she's on the other side of the world. So…she's given us the go-ahead to organise our own dresses.' It hadn't taken much to persuade Soraya to change her plans for the bridal party last minute, because she was the kind of sister, the kind of person, who would rather see everyone happy than concentrate on what she wanted. She'd insisted she wasn't giving up her childhood dreams of how her wedding should look and all that mattered was that Isolde and Raed's family were there and comfortable in their roles. Although Isolde had to promise that their outfits would be tasteful and hers in particular would not contravene any decency laws.

'I can choose my own dress?'

'Better than that. We're going to design them. I'm quite handy with a sewing machine. We're free to accessorise how we want, and that includes your wheelchair. The only caveat is that we don't upstage the bride.'

Both Isolde and Soraya thought that if Farah was more involved in deciding what to wear she might be more relaxed about the whole affair. Isolde knew Amir wouldn't be happy about Farah being part of the ceremony if she was upset so it was important to get him on side too. After all, Isolde didn't want to be there on her own as the outsider she was. At least when she was with Amir and Farah she felt part of a family again. Something she hadn't realised she needed until Soraya moved away.

'Do I get to design my suit too?' Amir asked, apparently on board with the scheme.

Isolde clicked her tongue against her teeth. 'I'm afraid not. Soraya didn't trust you not to turn up in a purple velvet suit and top hat.'

Amir nodded. 'She knows me too well. We both know I would only show up the groom if I truly let my light shine.'

'Yeah, you're in a sackcloth and ashes. Whereas I and Miss Farah will be resplendent in chiffon.' Isolde took Farah by the hand and twirled her around in her wheelchair, the little girl's smile telling her it would all be worth the effort.

It was going to take some work to make dresses good enough to stand up to scrutiny at a royal wedding but she knew she could do it. With money tight when they were growing up, she'd been the one able to mend their clothes or customise stuff they'd found in second-hand shops. Her quirky sense of style had been part of what made her...her. It was being with Olly, conforming to his ideas of how she should look and behave that had stolen away that part of her identity. Since working full-time at the hospital she hadn't had much chance to break free from her conventional work clothes. It might be nice to rediscover that creative side of her again.

'I've brought some magazines, paper and pencils so we can get cracking any time you're ready, Farah.' Isolde fetched the shoulder bag she'd brought with her from the kitchen but she looked to Amir before she produced the contents, looking for his approval.

His response was to swipe everything off the coffee table and pull it closer to Farah. He was an exceptional father, and it wasn't lost on Isolde that he was content to let her be exactly who she was without trying to temper her behaviour either. She hadn't believed men like that existed. If she'd known perhaps she wouldn't have wasted years of her life on someone who needed to change her. It was just as well Amir came with more baggage and responsibilities than a bohemian spirit like her could ever be comfortable with, or else her vow off men might be in jeopardy.

Amir sat back and watched as Isolde and Farah let their imaginations run loose. It was nice to see his daughter engaged again and having fun. Too much of her young life recently had been spent dealing with things no child should ever have to go through. The trauma of the accident, losing her mother, and her subsequent struggle to walk again had robbed her of her childhood. Isolde seemed to understand what Farah needed, both inside and outside the hospital. She was the only health professional his daughter had really bonded with, who didn't patronise her or push her further than she was ready to go. Isolde took things at Farah's pace and he was grateful for it. Especially now seeing her having fun and laughing again.

'I think fairy wings might be pushing it a little bit, Farah,' he said, peering over her shoulder at the sketch she'd made, still aware that this was Soraya and Raed's day and an important one for their country. There was a fine line between keeping his daughter happy and not wishing to embarrass the family. Anything too over the top ran the risk of drawing the kind of negative attention they were all hoping to protect Farah from in the first place. It was only the crestfallen look on her face, erasing the smile Isolde had managed to put there, that made him regret saying anything.

Isolde lifted the drawing Farah had made and held it up, tilting her head to one side as she studied it. 'You know, I think this would look good at the evening reception. Some glitter and sequins and you're ready to party. Plus, there won't be any cameras there so we can wear what we like.'

She gave Amir a pointed look. He wasn't sure if it was a signal for him to back off out of this project, or to let him know she had it all in hand. Either way he was happy to let her take the lead when the spark was so evidently back in Farah's eyes.

'Maybe I'll get that purple velvet suit for that,' he jested, doing his best to get back into everyone's good books after inadvertently putting a dampener on their fun.

'Or we could design you a Farah and Isolde original,' Isolde suggested, but that mischievous twinkle in her blue eyes offered a challenge he knew he wasn't prepared to meet.

'I don't think I'm ready for that. I think one

maverick in the family is more than enough. Concentrate on Farah's outfit, and yours, and I'll be content to blend into the background.' He could only imagine the horrors Isolde and his daughter would come up with for him if left to their own devices, and wasn't brave enough to be styled by either of them for this very public event. It would be his first official appearance since his wife's death and he didn't particularly want to draw any more attention than was necessary from the press.

'Spoilsport. Though I suppose it gives us more time to concentrate on our fabulous outfits, doesn't it, Farah?'

Farah nodded in agreement and Amir was reminded of the days when his wife and daughter used to team up to get their own way. It seemed such a long time ago now since they'd taken family votes on important issues such as what ice-cream flavour to buy, or whether or not Farah got to stay up late. All of which had been pointless anyway because his daughter had usually got her own way, but he knew that by getting her mother's support it had given her a sense of solidarity, and the feeling that she was getting one over on her father.

These days it was difficult to get her engaged in anything and he'd had to make all the decisions for her. Isolde was giving her back that sense of control in her life. It might only be over something as small as designing her own dress, but taking an interest in something again meant so much. They both had Isolde to thank for that when she'd obviously gone to great lengths to make this happen. He was sure it hadn't been easy to convince a bride to hand over the decision-making on the bridesmaids' outfits. The Yarrow sisters really were remarkable women.

'I'm sure you'll both look beautiful and have all the men falling at your feet.'

Isolde gave a brittle laugh. 'No, thanks. The last thing I need in my life is another man. Although I think I need to remind my darling sister of that too. My invitation came with a plus one. She must think that because she found love after her dud of an ex, the same will happen for me.'

Amir wondered who had put her off the idea of ever finding love and what horrible thing he'd done to Isolde to make her think she was better off alone. Especially when she was so full of love herself. He'd had his troubles with his wife later in the marriage but at least he'd experienced what it was to be part of a couple and a family. Although he wasn't in the market for a relationship again—his focus was on Farah's recovery—he didn't think he wanted to be on his own for ever. He was already feeling the loss of his brother and parents since they'd returned home, and once Farah was old enough to strike out on her own he knew he'd be lonely. Although they were close and she was his whole world, there was nothing he wanted more than for her to have her independence and a life that didn't revolve around her injury.

'Ah, they were more tactful with my invitation. Mine was for myself and Farah only. They mustn't think there's any hope for me finding love again at all.' His laugh was as humourless as Isolde's had been. Neither of them happy with their current situation. It wasn't that he was actively looking for another romantic partner, but he wasn't going to rule out the possibility.

Of course he missed his wife, was devastated by her death and the impact her loss had upon the family, but he wasn't grieving to the extent his brother seemed to think he was. He couldn't tell him otherwise. It seemed like a terrible betrayal to tell anyone that his marriage had been on the rocks at the time of his wife's death. He wanted people to remember her fondly. Yet he felt like a fraud because he hadn't been in love with her the way everyone thought when she died. And although there had been little love to keep him warm at night, he hadn't wanted the scandal of a divorce to rock his family. He'd been prepared to sacrifice his happiness to protect the monarchy, to keep up that front of stability. She hadn't.

It was something he could never share, in order to protect her memory, and Farah's feelings. Not to mention the whole family. That didn't mean he wasn't consumed by guilt over the lies, and the secret he knew he had to keep.

'I'm sure that's not the case. They probably didn't want to upset you, that's all. Hey, if we're both minus significant others why don't we go together? I'll get Soraya to make sure we're seated together so we don't have to make awkward small talk with random toffs. No offence,' she added, obviously including him in that description of the distinguished wedding guests.

'Some taken,' he said with a smile as Farah cheered the idea that Isolde should accompany them.

It was clear that Isolde had some qualms about the day too, though she would likely never admit that she was worried about being out of place. Amir could see why she might have some reservations when she wasn't used to the kind of lifestyle, and the kind of people that would be in attendance. As someone who didn't always appear to follow the usual social niceties, she might stand out in the crowd, though that made her exactly who she was, and why he liked her. Isolde was honest and forthright, qualities he appreciated, in a world where people constantly seemed to be trying to be something they weren't. Him included. It had taken him a long time to realise he couldn't please everyone all of the time, and he didn't want her to think she had to start.

'It's not quite the proposal your brother offered my sister. I don't want us to fake a romance or anything. Maybe we can just go together, as friends.' Isolde was clarifying the situation so there was no doubt that their relationship was probably for Farah's benefit as much as his. He knew how much she liked Isolde so it wouldn't be fair to let her think anything else was going on between them, or that Isolde was a replacement for her mother. When she put it so plainly he didn't see a problem. They were company for each other. All three of them.

'Just friends. I think we can manage that. We seem to be doing okay so far.'

Isolde leaned her head briefly against his shoulder in a gesture of said friendship. It was settled, they would be attending the royal wedding as a strictly platonic couple.

Now all he had to do was reconcile that idea with his treacherous body, which had reacted to her touch as a lot more than just a friend.

CHAPTER THREE

'THIS LOOKS LIKE PARADISE,' Isolde commented, not for the first time. It had been three weeks since the video call with Soraya. They'd kept in touch with texts and emails about the dresses, but she was glad she was here in Zaki to finally see her in person.

From the moment the turquoise water, golden sands and swaying palm trees of Zaki had come into view, she'd felt as though she were in another world. Even the air was different—it smelled clean and fresh, and felt warm on her skin.

'I suppose it does compared to the city, though we're kind of used to it. Before the accident we often travelled over from London as a family. We had always planned to move back here permanently. I just wanted Farah to have a taste of normal life before the madness kicked in and we took up our royal duties. She was supposed to have an education in England first, a childhood not blighted by media intrusion, or responsibility to an entire country. Things didn't work out that way…' Amir's voice trailed off and she could tell he was disappearing back into that abyss of grief that had robbed him and Farah of so much.

'I know, and I'm sorry. Thank you for doing this with me. I'm so out of my comfort zone.' She tried to get him to refocus on the present, not only for Raed and Soraya's sake, but for his and Farah's too. They needed a break from all the heartache and pain they'd gone through in London, and, though they'd be returning to continue Farah's treatment, father and daughter deserved a holiday of sorts.

'You'll be fine,' Amir assured her. 'You're a VIP now. Enjoy it.'

'That's easier said than done when you're not used to this pampered lifestyle.' There wasn't a lot Isolde wasn't willing to tackle— a product of an upbringing by a fierce older sister—but this change of pace was a lot for her to take.

After their long—first-class—flight, where she'd been treated like royalty along with her travelling companions, they were now in the back of a limousine rushing towards the royal palace. She was beginning to wish she hadn't indulged in the complimentary champagne quite so much.

It was easy to forget this was the life her sister was now part of when they lived so far apart. She'd only had a very small taste of the family's importance when they'd been trying so hard to protect the King from press intrusion after his heart attack. It made her wonder, not for the first time, about what Amir and Farah had gone through after the car accident that had taken his wife, Farah's mother, from them.

Even now, over a year later, Farah had been hesitant about travelling in the car. Something that must be a daily occurrence. Amir had gently coaxed her in, reminding her that he was with her and promising to keep her safe.

Isolde had only heard snippets about what had happened from Farah during their physio sessions, and a little of what Soraya knew, but it would have been unprofessional and immoral to ask her any more about it. The little girl had understandably been traumatised, her mother apparently dying upon impact, leaving Farah scared, in pain and alone until the paramedics and fire brigade had arrived on scene to remove her from the vehicle. Given the lengths Raed had gone to—faking an engagement to her sister to put the press off the scent of a story during their father's illness—she could only imagine how intrusive they'd been in the aftermath of the crash.

Amir was fiercely protective of his daughter, and rightly so when she only had one parent looking out for her now. Isolde had been that lost and frightened little girl once when she'd lost both parents and she knew having one strong role model made all the difference. It couldn't have been easy for them to come back here either, knowing there would be talk about them in the press and attention drawn to Farah's condition, but Amir would never let anything happen to Farah when she'd already been through so much. Isolde was simply hanging onto his coat-tails, hoping he would protect her too.

She knew she wasn't everyone's cup of tea, and, though Amir's family had been lovely, not everyone would have time for a commoner like her. While it didn't usually bother her, she didn't want to show Soraya up, or her new family.

Even thinking of Raed and his parents as Soraya's new family made her tear up. It was silly when they were both grown women, and she'd been the one to tell Soraya to go after Raed when he'd gone home to take up his royal role again and left his life in London behind. She wanted her big sister to be happy, but she'd also never been without her support and she couldn't help but feel the same abandonment she'd gone through after her parents had died. At least she was going to see Soraya soon. She was tempted to hug her and never let her go.

As the fairy-tale vision of the palace appeared before them, all arches and columns, tiles and intricate sculpture, the wealth divide was more apparent than ever. Isolde took a deep, shaky breath.

'We're here. Relax, you've met the family before, and Farah and I will be around if you need us.' Amir reached across the back seat to give her hand a squeeze.

'I'm scared too,' Farah admitted as they entered through the golden gates of the palace grounds. They drove into a courtyard, dominated by a huge octagonal water feature, surrounded by perfectly manicured shrubbery.

Amir took her hand too. 'I know it's been

a while since you've been here too, and circumstances are different. Just remember this is your family home and you're entitled to be here.

'You too,' he said to Isolde as she opened her mouth to comment otherwise.

She knew this had to be difficult for him too, but she supposed this was a joyous occasion for their siblings. Soraya deserved happiness and Isolde knew if Soraya thought for a second that her little sister wasn't happy she would focus on that rather than her own wedding day. After a lifetime of letting her big sister look after her, it was time for Isolde to reverse their roles.

'I think we should probably keep all of this to ourselves. Raed and Soraya don't need to know we're worried about everything. They've enough to deal with. I say we make a pact that all three of us face whatever is to come, together, and if there are any problems we discuss it with the group rather than take it to the happy couple. Deal?' She looked at Amir and Farah in turn for their support.

'Deal.'

'Deal.'

They each joined hands in solidarity and Isolde knew they'd get through this if they all stayed together. It was once the wedding was over and they were back in England, back to their own lives, that she'd have to worry about getting too close. Until then, she needed her team together.

'Isolde!' Soraya swamped her in a hug before she'd barely set foot onto the marble floor of the palace. The familiar warmth and scent of her big sister was something she'd missed for so long. Isolde let herself be completely immersed in that feeling of unconditional love that she'd been without for six months.

'Brother.' Raed walked over to Amir and gave him a quick hug in a more reserved display of affection.

'Fa-Fa!' Raed turned his attention to his niece, giving her a bear hug before taking off running with her down the hallway, her squeals of delight echoing around the walls.

It made Isolde feel less self-conscious about clinging onto Soraya for so long. Clearly family was a big deal here too.

'It's so lovely to see you all.' The Queen came to greet them, looking resplendent in yellow silk, and once more Isolde was torn about whether or not to curtsey. The last time they'd met she'd made a botched job of it and been told it wasn't necessary. She supposed they were going to be family soon enough and she couldn't go around curtseying to everyone all the time or her knees would soon give up. Instead, she reached out and shook her hand, finally leaving go of Soraya.

'Thank you for having me, Djamila.' Amir and Farah had every right to be here but Isolde couldn't help but feel as though she was imposing on the family's generous hospitality.

'I'm sure you're all exhausted after the journey. We've given you rooms together if you'd like to get settled in.'

'Thank you.'

'I can show you up,' Soraya offered, holding tightly to Isolde's arms. 'I can't wait to tell you about all of the work we're doing out here.'

Isolde had heard all about their charity projects on the numerous telephone calls they'd shared since Soraya left the country, but Soraya's excitement at actually getting to show Isolde the work they'd done was tangible. She was proud of her big sis, but at the same time it was a reminder that she had a life away from her. Excitement and glamour Isolde could only dream about. She went to work and came home to her empty flat. The only excitement had been the pizza night at Amir's house weeks ago, and that had been to make sure Farah was comfortable with her role in the wedding.

Although they'd achieved their objective, it had given Isolde a ton of work to do on the dresses, which Soraya still had to approve. It was a lot of pressure to keep everyone happy and she was beginning to realise the burden of responsibility her sister had been carrying all these years. She deserved every bit of luxury provided to her by her new family circumstances out here, though Soraya would never be someone who would simply sit back while others struggled. Which no doubt Isolde would see for herself later on.

Amir and Farah had disappeared into the room next door, led by Raed, and Soraya opened the door to Isolde's room. It was bigger than her entire flat.

'Not too shabby,' she said, taking in the sight. 'I might need a map to find my way around though.'

'Isn't it amazing? Apparently Amir specifically asked Raed to save this room for you because it has the best view.' Soraya moved to the double window and opened it up onto a balcony.

'It's beautiful.' For the first time in her life Isolde was truly awestruck. She had a clear view, not only of the palace gardens, but also of the stunning hills in the distance. It was a little paradise, and the wrought-iron table and chairs would be perfect for her to come and chill out day or night. She was already imagining having breakfast out here listening to the birds in the trees tomorrow morning. Different from the sounds of traffic and construction work on the streets of London. Another reminder that she and Soraya now lived in completely different worlds.

'I think this used to be Amir's room before he moved to England. Not that there's any sign of him in it. I wonder if they redecorated it after he left.' Soraya looked around as though she was seeing it for the first time too, picking up one of the dozens of scatter cushions lined up on the huge bed.

Isolde glanced around and saw the framed photograph of Amir and Raed in pride of place on the nightstand, and the handmade aeroplane models dotted around the bookcase, and knew exactly whose room this had been. 'I can see his fingerprints all over it. It's just like his living room.'

Soraya arched an eyebrow at her. 'You've been at his house?'

Isolde got the impression Soraya and Raed had been trying to matchmake ever since that afternoon tea they'd shared together, simply because she and Amir had an easy, comfortable relationship. Mostly because they were friends and knew there was no more to it than that when they both had so much baggage. They didn't need complicated romantic entanglements when they were both struggling to move on from their last partners, but they did enjoy one another's company. It wasn't so easy trying to get that point across to anyone else.

'Yes. I've been working with Farah on getting these dresses ready for the wedding, remember?' She wouldn't mention being invited over for dinner. That was asking for trouble.

'Uh-huh. You two seem to be spending a lot of time together recently, and now he's your plus one?'

'Listen, sis, I get you want me to have my own happy ever after, but you're seriously looking at the wrong girl if you think I'm going to give up my life to play stepmother to someone else's kid. You know that just isn't me. I'm done being the little housewife and enjoying being footloose and fancy free.'

Well, she would, if she had any kind of social life. Unfortunately when she'd settled down with Olly she'd lost touch with her more…bohemian friends. Now if she was lucky it was a quick drink after work with her colleagues, or a takeaway at a friend's house.

Soraya snorted. 'I'm not sure you were ever the little housewife.'

Isolde lifted one of the silk cushions off the bed and threw it at her. 'You know what I mean. Olly wanted someone to conform to society's rules and settle down with a couple of kids. I'm just not the maternal type.'

'Really? You seem to be doing a pretty good job with Farah, as far as I can see.'

'That's different. She's a patient, and only family by your marriage, not mine. So stop trying to make something out of nothing.' She grabbed another cushion and launched it, then another, until Soraya began to fight back, and the floor became littered with the debris of their childish fight.

Eventually they both collapsed onto the

mattress, breathless and smiling. 'I've missed you, Isolde.'

'I've missed you too.'

'But don't think I'm giving up on this. After all, Amir sacrificed his room for you.'

Isolde reached across for the last remaining cushion and batted it onto Soraya's face. 'Enough.'

She was touched by the gesture, that he'd allowed her to encroach on such a personal space so she could enjoy the view better. No doubt his way of saying thank you for helping him with Farah, not that she expected anything for it. She enjoyed her time with the little girl; it gave her a chance to indulge her inner child, although Soraya might say she'd never really grown up. That might have been true at one time but since Soraya had moved here with Raed, Isolde had had no choice but to grow up. It wasn't all it was cracked up to be. Although helping out with Farah had given her a peek at what life might have been like if she had decided to settle down and have kids with Olly.

She saw the worrying Amir did over his daughter, and the responsibility he took in trying to make her happy, because Isolde had been living it with him during these wedding preparations. But the reward of seeing Farah smile made it all worthwhile. Isolde knew because she'd been working towards the same goal. What they all wanted more than anything was to see her walk again, to have her childhood back, and not to have to have physiotherapy or surgery. Unfortunately, there was still a long way to go for that to happen, but that didn't stop Isolde from trying to get her there.

She was close to all her young patients, all of them special to her in different ways, and she did her best to improve their quality of life through their sessions. However, Farah held a bigger piece of her heart. Even before the family connection, when Soraya had stepped in to be Raed's fake fiancée, Isolde had had a real bond with Farah. Perhaps it was the loss of her parents at such a young age that made her relate to that lost, frightened little girl who'd come through the trauma of a crash that took her mother from her.

She knew what it was like to have her whole world upended like that, not knowing what the future held without a mother to turn to. It was scary, and that was without the added stress of not being able to walk. Farah was brave and strong, just like her father.

Isolde had to admit that she had a soft spot for him too. Amir had a quiet strength and seemed to just get on with everything that fate threw at him. He reminded her a little of Soraya that way. He'd been dealt a very difficult hand but ploughed on trying to do his best for everyone. She was sure it wasn't easy when he was grieving the loss of his wife and he had his daughter's troubles to worry about. It gave Isolde a new perspective on having grown up expecting Soraya to simply deal with everything that came along because she was so capable. She could see now the strength of character it took to do that in the face of so many challenges, and she'd let Isolde sail through life without a care in the world, oblivious to her own emotional struggles. Exactly what Amir was trying to do now for Farah.

Isolde wasn't the girl's mother, but she felt a responsibility to try and make her happy too. Even if that came in the form of her dressmaking skills, rather than her medical ones for now.

'I just want you to be happy, Isolde.' Soraya

rolled over onto her side and fixed her with her 'serious big sister' look.

'I am,' she lied. It wasn't that she was sad about anything in particular, she simply hadn't found anything in her life that made her happy the way Soraya was out here. And she was lonely. She didn't know what she would do if she didn't have Amir and Farah to call on every now and then. Although once the wedding was over she wouldn't have that to use as an excuse to see them any more. Perhaps she needed to spread her wings and go travelling. She'd never wanted to settle down, so maybe keeping on the move was the way forward.

'Welcome to our Home from Home centre. A place where young carers can hang out and have fun. We've got counsellors on hand for anyone who needs a chat, and we're currently offering cooking lessons for families on a budget.'

It was clear Soraya was very excited about their new venture as Amir and Isolde struggled to keep up with her on their way into the new building.

'This must have taken some planning,' he said to Raed, who had hung back and let his fiancée take the lead in showing them around. Farah was tired and had remained at the palace with his parents, while Amir and Isolde tagged along on the tour.

'We just transferred the idea from the London branch. All Soraya's idea of course, but we both come here when we can to help out.' Raed had contributed heavily to the funding of the UK project in an attempt to get Soraya on board with the fake-fiancée ruse at the time. Amir had since learned that the cause was one very close to her heart because of the time she'd spent caring for her parents before they died, and afterwards raising Isolde on her own. She was a good influence on the family, reminding them how privileged they were in their position, and that they could make a difference. Amir was glad his brother and soon-to-be sister-in-law were still able to make such a huge difference to people's lives out here. One of the reasons they'd all gone into the medical field was to help people and this way Raed and Soraya got to continue their good work.

'How are you funding it?' he asked, curious to find out how they kept it maintained now that it was up and running.

'I mean, we have all sorts of financial managers involved, but we've also got lots of donations and sponsorship secured. As long as we keep the profile raised in the press, we should be good.' Raed was a man of his word and Amir knew he wouldn't simply walk away from a project when he tired of it.

Although he'd resisted coming back here to take up his royal duties again, when the time had come, he'd stepped up. With their father ill at the time, and Amir unable to return because of Farah, Raed had left the life he had built for himself in London to do the right thing by everyone else. He'd been willing to sacrifice his own happiness for that of the country. Thank goodness he'd met Soraya, who'd been willing to stand by him. They deserved all the happiness they'd found together.

'We'd like you to meet some of our young people.' Soraya walked them past the bank of computer games and a pool table, waving at the groups of teens congregated, chatting and laughing.

It was a bright modern space littered with oversized beanbags to sit on and plenty of activities to take part in. Soraya pointed to a couple of doors off to the side, which were apparently off limits to them at present.

'That's our counsellor's office, and next door is the quiet space where kids can come and do their homework. Not all the children have a place at home where they can study so they come here.' It was clear Soraya had tried to cover all the needs of their young carers, probably because she'd been the child who'd needed a space to hang out, to study without interruption, and free from responsibility.

Isolde had told him everything Soraya had done for her growing up, a very different childhood from the one he and Raed had experienced. Though it hadn't been easy because of the pressures they'd been under as young children to be well behaved in the public spotlight, Amir was thankful for the material things they'd never had to worry about. Emotionally, however, it could be argued that their needs had been as neglected as these young children. That was part of the reason he'd wanted Farah's early schooling to take place in England, out of the spotlight, and where he was able to devote more time to her than his parents ever had to him.

'Is there somewhere for little sisters who are oblivious to all the grown-up struggles their siblings are going through to go so they don't feel left out?' Isolde took her sister's hand and it was obvious she understood things now in a different light. He knew how much she was struggling without her family, the same way he was, but she was putting Soraya's feelings before her own. Showing a real maturity for someone who often said she'd never grown up.

'Come here and I'll show you.' Soraya took her by the hand and led her to a long table where the kids were getting stuck into arts and crafts, glitter and glue everywhere.

'Hi,' Isolde said and immediately took a seat to see what everyone was making while Soraya and Raed spoke to some of the adult leaders.

Spotting the empty seat beside Isolde, Amir sat down too, wishing they had brought Farah along and tried to get her involved too. He'd seen how engaged she'd been with Isolde over the whole dress-designing sessions, clearly a creative soul like her mentor.

'So, what are you making here?' Isolde took a fresh sheet of paper from the pile in the middle of the table and glanced at the work the young boy next to her was doing, his tongue sticking out in concentration.

'We're making pictures showing our wishes,'

he said, grabbing a glue stick and some pipe cleaners.

'I've made a unicorn,' the little girl on the other side of Isolde said, proudly showing off her drawing, which was little more than a squiggle saturated with silver glitter and glue, but which she was clearly very proud of.

'That's an excellent unicorn,' Isolde said, giving her a thumbs up for her efforts. 'I think I'll do a beach scene.'

'Is that where you wish you were?' Amir asked, curious about the things Isolde wanted in life because she never discussed her needs, only everyone else's. It struck him that since they'd first met, she'd always been working towards improving other people's lives. Not only her patients'. He knew she was missing her sister as much as he was missing his family, but Isolde hadn't told Soraya lest she upset her. She'd never once voiced dissatisfaction with her lot, but he couldn't help but feel she needed more.

'Some days,' she said on a wistful sigh.

'Maybe we should gatecrash the honeymoon,' he suggested, only half joking.

'I think I'd prefer something more low-key.'

'A desert island perhaps?'

'Definitely.'

It had been a long time since he and Farah had been on a holiday, or had any time out from their recent stresses. This trip didn't count, since they would be under a spotlight for the whole duration, and had a duty not to mess up in the eyes of the world's press. A nice quiet break on an isolated beach in the sun actually sounded like heaven. He was sure Farah would enjoy it too. Though he suspected asking Isolde to join them might be pushing the boundaries of their friendship a little far, he couldn't imagine going on such a trip without her now.

She brought him such peace simply by being around he didn't know what he was going to do once the wedding was over and there was no longer any excuse for them to hang out. He supposed they'd still see each other at work, and any family occasions, but it wouldn't be the same as eating pizza in his kitchen.

The trouble was he didn't know how to tell her he wanted her to stay in his life without making things weird between them. She'd made it clear she didn't want to settle down, or have family of her own, so he knew that ruled him out even if he had held any romantic notions that they might end up as more than just friends. That was primarily what had held him back from looking at her as anything else, along with his need to protect Farah. She needed stability, not her father introducing women into her life that weren't going to be around for ever. Perhaps it was time they both got used to that idea before he got as attached to Isolde as Farah.

'What are you making, Amir? A picture of you in a pilot uniform?' she asked with a wink.

'I see you've discovered my penchant for all things aeronautical. Yes, in different circumstances perhaps I might've entertained the idea of becoming a pilot. Though I'm afraid I simply went for a sunny day in the park.' He put forward his efforts of a crayoned sun and tissue-paper grass illustrating his simple dream to a chorus of titters from unimpressed children around him. Clearly he wasn't the artistic one around here.

'Thanks for the room, by the way. It was very kind of you to give it up for me.' Isolde went off topic to acknowledge the gesture he'd made in an attempt to make her feel more at home.

'It was no problem. I thought you might

enjoy the view.' Amir knew what it was like feeling like an outsider in that vast mansion, and he was part of the family. His role had always been to stay in the background, supporting his older brother, like everyone else. He didn't resent Raed, he'd always admired him, but his parents tended to forget they had another child when they had spent their lives prepping Raed to be King. With the wedding coming up he didn't wish for Isolde to get lost in the noise too. At least if she had a quiet place to retreat to, a space to call her own, it might help to shield her from the pressures of royal life.

'I do. Much better than the one I have now,' she said, squinting at his picture. 'Although, if that's your big dream I think we're both in need of a sunny holiday.'

For a moment the idea that there might be a chance they would get to go on their dream vacation together seemed to hover in the air, at least as far as Amir was concerned. Then Isolde turned away, focusing on the children's artwork again, and the moment passed.

'So, what's your big dream?' he asked the little boy who was studiously sketching away next to him. This was why they were here, to interact with these children, not to get carried away with pipe dreams and what ifs.

'This is me in the hospital.' The boy pointed to the macabre stick figure stretched out on what he supposed to be a hospital bed, the strange vision causing Amir to furrow his brow. He was contemplating whether or not he should speak to one of the counsellors on the child's behalf when Raed walked over.

'Ah, I see you've met Fahid. Good.' Raed rested his hand on the child's back like a proud parent. 'This little man is not only caring for his sick, widowed mother, but he's also waiting for a lobectomy. He has benign tumours all over his lungs.'

As a thoracic surgeon, Amir knew what a lobectomy was, and he suspected that was why he was really here. He gave Raed the side-eye but his brother simply smiled and shrugged.

'Call it a working holiday,' he said, placing Fahid's drawing in front of him. Now he knew exactly what it depicted, Amir couldn't help but be affected. This child's dream was something he could help to achieve.

'How long's the waiting list?'

Raed held his gaze, communicating the importance of his participation in this scenario.

'Too long and his mother is worried sick because she can't do anything to help him. He lost his father a few years ago and they only have each other.'

'When I have my surgery I can play football with my friends again.' Fahid, seemingly oblivious to the background shenanigans, continued to colour, adding in a faceless surgeon he was likely hoping would miraculously cure him.

Amir thought of Farah, of the things she could no longer do, and how he wished he were in a position to change that. Now here he was able to make a difference to another child's life and he knew he couldn't go back home until he'd done his part.

'Send me his files,' he said gruffly to Raed, ticked off that he'd been manipulated in such an obvious way.

'It was lovely to meet you, Fahid, and everyone else.' He scraped back his chair and left the table.

'All you had to do was ask,' he hissed at Raed as he walked by, suddenly needing some air and time out from his brother's charity project.

'I'm sorry, brother—'

'Amir?'

He heard the concern in Raed and Isolde's voices behind him but he couldn't stop, he couldn't talk, because he was afraid of all that pain and emotion he'd been holding back since the aftermath of the accident.

It wasn't the idea of performing the routine procedure on Fahid that was causing him distress, or even the underhanded way his brother had gone about things. No, it was the fact no one, not even a surgeon as skilled as he, could fix his daughter so easily. He would do anything if Farah could have her life back with one simple operation. It didn't matter that her injuries were beyond anyone's capabilities, he still felt like a failure. As a father, and as a surgeon. It was his job to take care of Farah, to improve lives, and if anyone should be able to help her it should be him. If he was going to change a child's life, it should be his own.

He'd already failed his family when his wife had wanted a divorce. It was his fault she'd driven off in such a state that night because he wouldn't agree to it, that she'd crashed the car, and injured Farah, that she'd died. The only thing he could do to try and make things right was to help his daughter walk again and he couldn't even do that.

Seeing Fahid, the struggles he was having, and knowing that one operation could turn his life around, had brought all that guilt to the fore. He'd been trying to keep it at bay, focusing on Farah's recovery, afraid that he'd fall apart. She needed him to be strong. It was all he could do.

Right now he needed some space to get those defences back in place. He was already vulnerable, away from home, he and Farah in the spotlight for the first time since the accident, and battling this increasing need for Isolde in his life. The last thing he needed was a public emotional breakdown.

'I'll go.' Isolde touched Raed's arm, silently asking him not to go after his brother. She'd witnessed the exchange, seen the pained expression on Amir's face as he'd left, and knew he needed some space from everyone pressuring him. She hoped that didn't include her.

'Raed? What happened?' Soraya arrived on the scene having missed the exchange but Isolde was sure she knew what had Amir so riled. She doubted there was anything that went on in this centre that her sister wasn't aware of.

'I think hearing Fahid's story has probably made him think about Farah and wish he could make her life better with one simple procedure. Give him a moment. I'll go and check on him.' Isolde said her goodbyes to the kids and made her way towards the back door, which Amir had disappeared through only moments ago, hoping she wouldn't be intruding too much.

Given the scene she'd just witnessed, she figured the last thing he'd want was his brother following him, but she considered herself neutral in this sibling battle. She knew Raed and Soraya had meant well with this whole set-up, but she also knew how much Amir beat himself up every day about not being able to help Farah. It must have been hard for him to be rendered powerless when it came to his own daughter's health issues. Never more so than when he was reminded of the difference he could make to the quality of another child's life.

He was pacing up and down the car park at the back, his body so tense she was sure he was ready to snap in half at any given moment.

'Hey,' she said, tapping him on the shoulder to let him know she was there.

He whirled around, poised and ready for

combat. Then he saw her and she watched as all the fight left him, his shoulders falling and his fists unclenching. 'Sorry. I didn't realise it was you, Isolde.'

'I come in peace.' She held her hands up in surrender, finding some satisfaction in the half-smile she managed to raise.

'It's not your fault. It's not anyone's fault. Except mine,' he said cryptically, scrubbing his hands over his scalp.

'You can talk to me, Amir. I know there are things that are bothering us that we can't say to family, but we can confide in each other. We're both kind of floundering in the deep end at the moment.'

'It's not that I begrudge helping anyone on my time off, and not even that Racd tricked me into agreeing to do the surgery. Which, by the way, I would have done anyway if he'd asked.'

'I know that, and he knows that. Perhaps they simply wanted you to meet Fahid for yourself and understand the impact you could have on his life.'

'I guess so. It's just a reminder that I can't do anything for my own daughter. A few hours in an operating theatre with other people's children and I can give them their childhood back. Fahid's already lost his father, he's grieving and scared. Just like my Farah. I understand his mother's feelings of inadequacy but at least I can do something for their family. It doesn't matter how much time I devote to Farah, I can't do the same for her. I can't make her wish come true.' The pain was so obvious in his words, in his eyes, that it hurt to even watch him go through it. Isolde felt every bit as powerless as he did right now.

'You have done everything you possibly could, Amir, but you can't work miracles. I've seen you together and you are the best father that little girl could ever ask for.' She worked with a lot of families and not every parent was as present and involved as Amir in their child's treatment. But some things simply couldn't be fixed by sheer determination.

'You don't understand. All of this is my fault.' He threw up his hands and walked away. For a moment she thought he was going to leave the grounds altogether, away from the conversation. Instead, he moved over to the bench just outside the centre's doors.

Isolde followed him over and sat down, realising he wanted, needed, someone to talk to about whatever he'd been holding onto for all these months. She traced her fingers over the letters carved into the back of the seat.

'"Reflection." Couldn't be more apt, could it?'

'I don't know... *Guilt* might be more apt.' Amir leaned forward and rested his head in his hands and it was all she could do not to hug him. He looked like the loneliest man in the world and she wanted to remind him he wasn't. That she was here for him.

'What happened to Farah wasn't your fault. From what I heard you weren't even in the car that night.' It was natural for a parent to blame themselves when a child was hurt; she'd seen enough of that at the hospital. That level of responsibility was the reason she couldn't imagine ever having children of her own. It was heartbreaking to watch and she didn't think she could ever be the parent a child deserved. Watching Amir's guilt was proof of that. If a man who devoted his whole life to his daughter's well-being couldn't get things right, what hope did she have?

He lifted his head and turned his dark, sorrowful eyes onto her. 'I caused the accident. It's my fault Farah can't walk and that her mother's no longer around.'

'That's not—'

Amir interrupted another attempt to placate him with a bombshell that left Isolde temporarily speechless.

'She told me she wanted a divorce. I said I would never agree. It would cause too much of a scandal to my family. That's why she drove away with Farah, why she was so distracted. I was willing to force us both to stay in a loveless marriage, one where I obviously wasn't enough, to save face. It cost me everything. All I had to do was be brave and agree. Instead, I sent her to her death.'

By all accounts, including from his own family, he'd had the perfect marriage. She'd seen how devastated he'd been by the loss of his wife and she would never have guessed there had been any problems. Which explained why he felt as though he couldn't talk to anyone about it. She'd been around the royal family enough to know they didn't like to present anything other than a perfect front to the world. Apparently that extended to each other too, if he hadn't been able to reach out to his brother during all of this turmoil. It was clear by the way Raed had talked about the tragic loss of his sister-in-law in the past that he wasn't aware that their marriage had been in difficulty.

She supposed the same could have been said about the secrecy between her and Soraya when it came to their personal lives. Both had been going through their own relationship struggles and had neglected to turn to one another for support through fear of upsetting each other. Perhaps if they had they wouldn't have stayed in toxic relationships for as long as they had. If she'd known half of what Frank had been up to she wouldn't have hesitated in dragging her sister away from him. As it was she hadn't known until it was too late, until he'd taken everything from Soraya, and left her with nowhere to go except Isolde's spare room.

It was easy to get lost in a relationship, as if it were the only important thing in the world, making it difficult to let go. She'd lost her sense of self when she'd been with Olly, and would've done almost anything to keep him happy. Except have a family. It was only when he'd pushed that point that she'd realised how much of herself she'd compromised and finally woken up.

She supposed Amir hadn't reached that point, admitting things hadn't been good. Perhaps with a little time he would have, which was what made this all the more difficult. Now he never would, forever holding onto the fact his wife hadn't been happy. Afraid to tell anyone and taint her memory. Still, it didn't make him accountable for what had happened.

'You weren't the one driving, Amir,' she said softly. Feeling some level of guilt over the situation was understandable but it didn't make it justified. In the circumstances she would likely have felt the same way when she'd blamed herself for the end of her relationship with Olly, even though he'd known who she was when they'd got together. It must have been harder for Amir when he hadn't been able to vent to anyone about what had happened, how hurt he was. At least until now.

'I may as well have been. Although my driving was just one more thing she criticised.' When he talked about his wife now she could hear the hint of bitterness mixed with his grief. On the occasions when he had mentioned her, Isolde had always taken that faraway look as a longing for the life they'd had together. Now she thought it might be more about regret. The kind she experienced in moments of vulnerability that made her think about the time she'd wasted with Olly, and the wish that things could somehow have worked out differently. Simply because sometimes being on her own had seemed harder than staying in a troubled relationship.

'I'm sorry you weren't on good terms when she died. I think it's conflicted your emotions over what happened. Really, your marriage ending and the crash are two different events.' And she suspected that neither were his fault.

'I should have just put on my happy face the way I'm supposed to and agreed, then she would never have driven off like that in such a rage. That's what the royal family are supposed to do, we just grit our teeth and bear whatever life throws at us. It's what I did my whole childhood.'

'That's not healthy either, Amir.' Isolde thought of Soraya, the way she'd dealt with everything from their parents' ill health, to working non-stop to provide for the family without complaint. It was noble, but ultimately had led her to believe that her feelings didn't matter. That she should keep everything to herself and concentrate on making other people happy. Something Isolde realised she'd tried to emulate with Olly. It was time someone broke out of this self-sacrificing cycle because, in the end, no one was happy.

'Yeah, I don't want Farah to grow up thinking that way, believing she can't be who she wants to be through fear of upsetting anyone. I let a toxic relationship go on too long, fostering the same kind of atmosphere I had growing up in my own house. I had to be the best son to keep my parents happy because they were so focused on Raed they didn't need me causing them any trouble. That carried over into my marriage, trying not only to be the best son, but to be the best husband too. I thought that meant clinging onto a marriage that wasn't good for any of us. It caused Farah irreparable damage.'

His voice broke then, his daughter his apparent kryptonite. Yet Isolde knew he'd done the right thing. She hoped with time he'd realise that too.

'You didn't do anything wrong. It's easy to blame ourselves for things going wrong. Believe me, I did the same thing in my relationship. I was so used to having Soraya protecting me and looking after me I guess I was afraid to be on my own. So, when she married Frank, and I met Olly, I tried to be everything he wanted. I didn't want anyone else to leave me, so I tried to be what he needed. I gave up a transient life, living in the moment, to settle down with a steady job. Now, ironically, it's that stable life that's my safety net. The security of my career and home was all I could rely on once Olly was out of my life. Then Soraya's marriage ended and she needed somewhere to go. For once I was able to do something for her. So I stayed put, stayed still, and tried to be the responsible adult she needed me to be.'

She believed now her young carefree years, which she realised now had come at the expense of her sister's freedom, had been a direct response to her parents' deaths. A child who'd seen how short and fragile life was at first hand and had wanted to enjoy every second of it. She missed that naïve existence, although it had left Soraya to carry the burden of responsibility alone, and she didn't think she could be that selfish any more.

'I can't imagine anyone trying to tell you what to do.' Amir smiled at her and she wished she'd always been the person he apparently thought her to be—strong, independent, and nobody's fool. It would've saved her a lot of heartache.

'Yes, well, I was young, naïve, and eager

to please. Thank goodness I saw the error of my ways.' It was her turn to smile, trying to lighten the mood when discussing a dark period in her past. It seemed only fair when Amir had been so open with her on a subject that had not only been causing him untold pain, but was also something he hadn't shared even with family.

She was privileged he trusted her with the information and it only went to prove how close they'd become in such a short span of time. If it weren't for the upcoming wedding, and her need to be around someone who understood her, she would have heeded the warning signs. As it was, she didn't want to see or hear them at a time when she needed all the friends she could get.

'What was the wake-up call for you?'

'That would be when he wanted me to give up my new job and have his babies. That was one thing I wasn't prepared to compromise on. Soraya and I went through a lot as kids and I think some of that could've been prevented. My parents refused to give up smoking even though they knew it was killing them, that lung cancer would take them away from their two young daughters. Okay, so the damage had been done long before we arrived, but they might have been able to buy some extra time if they'd thought of us. It might seem selfish to some, but I don't want to be responsible for bringing more lives into the world only to let them down like that.'

'That's not selfish, that's self-preservation. I think the things we've done, the way we've acted, has been out of a need for survival when we didn't have anyone else to protect us. Have you ever told Soraya any of this?'

She shook her head. 'I was enough of a burden to her growing up without adding my orphan issues to her load.'

Her shaky smile wasn't enough to convince him to drop the subject.

'Well, I'm here, and I know what a wonderful, generous, loving person you are. I'm sure you'd be an amazing mother, and yeah, we make mistakes as parents, but our children love us unconditionally. Thank goodness.'

Isolde looked into Amir's eyes and saw that same feeling of loneliness and fear she'd been living with since she lost her parents. He'd been through a lot after his loss too, because of the secrets he'd been forced to keep, and the front he'd had to adopt for Farah's sake.

It brought back those memories of whispered voices and people crying, no one willing to tell her what was going on because she was 'too young to understand'. Only to be told later that her parent had gone, leaving her more confused. She'd been through that twice in barely a year, left with just her big sister to comfort her and take care of her. Yet she'd never been able to voice the impact the loss of her parents had on her until now because she'd known Soraya had been through much worse, having to deal with everything left behind. This was the first time she'd been allowed to express that fear, and have it validated. Amir understood and it opened the floodgates for all of the confusing emotions she'd felt at that time to come flooding to the fore, finally grieving for her parents and the loss of a future with them. To her horror, her eyes began to fill with tears and her bottom lip started to wobble.

'I wish I'd known you back then,' she said on a sob.

Amir reached out and brushed his thumb across her trembling bottom lip. 'You have me now.'

When he leaned in and pressed his mouth against hers it felt like the most natural thing in the world. His kiss, so tender and comforting, was somewhere she wanted to stay for ever. She wanted to believe that she did have him, that this could last for ever. It was the first time since Soraya had moved away that she didn't feel alone.

Then Amir stood up and walked away, reminding her that any sense of security was only fleeting. In the end, everyone left her.

CHAPTER FOUR

IDIOT. AMIR WAS still chastising himself days later for crossing the line with Isolde and kissing her. Every time he saw her he remembered feeling her soft lips against his, the taste of her, and felt the need to kiss her all over again. It had been an error of judgement in a moment of weakness, when they'd both been vulnerable and in need of some emotional support. A mistake because nothing could come of it.

Even if he weren't a widower with a young daughter he needed to focus on, or a member of the royal family Isolde's sister was about to marry into, a relationship wasn't something he should even be considering. Not with someone like Isolde, who'd made it clear settling down with a family was not something the future held for her. He and Farah were a ready-made family and, like Isolde, he wasn't about to compromise that status for anything. First and foremost he was a father and wouldn't jeopardise that for any romantic interlude. He was never going to be the type of man to embark on a fling, and he wouldn't bring just any woman into his daughter's life. Isolde especially made things difficult when she was already such a big part of Farah's life. There was no point in starting something when she'd been very clear she didn't want the responsibility that came with being part of a family unit. Yet he didn't want to lose her out of their lives altogether.

He didn't know if it was too late to make amends when she hadn't shown up at the hospital for Fahid's operation. Raed was here supporting them both, as was Soraya, though she'd gone to get some refreshments while they waited for the time slot in the operating theatre.

'I'm sorry again, Amir. I didn't mean to upset you. I should have gone about things differently.' Raed apologised for the umpteenth time since the day in the centre.

'It's all right. I suppose I'm still trying to get used to the fact I'm not superhuman, and I can't fix everything, or everybody. Fahid reminded me of Farah, having lost a parent, and I simply yearned to be able to make a difference to my daughter's life in the same way. I should be grateful for the things I can do. Now you're back in the arms of the family, carrying out the role I couldn't, it's just as well I have a medical career to fall back on.'

He was only partly joking. Although as the eldest son, Raed was always meant to be next in line to the throne, Amir had been preparing himself to take over for a while. When his brother had first voiced his plans to surrender his position in the royal family, Amir had thought it was his time to shine, to prove to his parents and his wife that he was worthy of his position in the family too. More than a spare son should anything happen to the heir. He guessed he was wrong. Although, with Farah's future uncertain, he supposed it relieved some of the pressure that otherwise would have fallen on his shoulders.

'I'm sorry, brother. With everything that happened, I never thought to ask how you felt about anything, or what your long-term plans are.'

It was true, they hadn't had an honest conversation about the situation as a family since the afternoon they'd come up with the 'fake fiancée' cover story, inveigling Soraya into their mess. Amir supposed because no one wanted to upset their father, who, though much stronger than he had been, was still recovering from his heart attack and subsequent operation.

Although the rest of his family were living in a different country, Amir liked to think that everything that had happened had brought them closer. All were concerned about him and Farah checking in regularly with them, and asking about his work along with her progress. Perhaps the chasm had been all in his head growing up, and he'd been the one constantly comparing himself to his elder brother. They hadn't been particularly close when they'd both lived in London, busy with their own lives and futures. Now it seemed the losses, and near losses, they'd suffered had made every one of them realise how lucky they were to have one another.

He knew he'd always have a family home to return to, a lifestyle that meant never having to worry about money, if he ever decided to return and look after Farah full-time. His family would be supportive of whatever he chose, he knew that, and it was a comfort to him on the days when he did feel alone and powerless.

'I'm not sure myself. I don't want to uproot Farah when she's still receiving treatment so I guess life in London goes on as usual for now. Long term, I might come back to Zaki. That was always the plan, and now, with everyone else back here, life is kind of lonely.'

It was the first time he'd admitted that to his brother, always wanting to be seen as strong and capable by his family. Something that didn't really seem to matter any more. He'd failed in his duty as a son, a prince, a husband, and as a father. The best he could do now was be there for his daughter, come what may.

'I'm sorry we're not there for you, Amir. You know you and Farah are always welcome to come home. I'm sure Mother and Father would be glad to have us all here. But you do what you have to do.' Raed wasn't one to say things he didn't mean and it meant a lot to Amir that his brother would happily welcome him back.

He'd always looked up to his older brother. When he'd seen the difference Raed had been making in the medical field, he'd followed him into the profession. It had seemed to him then that if he wasn't going to be an important figurehead in the family, a medical career could be as rewarding, and it had been. He'd even been able to work in Zaki for a time, making a difference to many patients and their families, before Farah had been born.

The news of Raed's intended surrender of his position had given him a renewed sense of purpose and he'd been preparing to take the role himself. Deep down he had hoped it would help save his marriage, that returning to their home country in prominent roles would make his wife look more favourably upon him. But it hadn't been enough. Then the crash and his father's ill health had changed all their lives and made them reassess everything. He'd become a little more sensitive in the interim, it would seem.

'As long as you don't spring any more surprises on me...'

'Don't worry, I've had very strong words with my husband about being tactful in the future. We had discussed the possibility of getting you involved, but I certainly wasn't part of the ambush.' Soraya appeared beside them carrying coffee. She'd been mortified by the events of that day at the centre, apologising for both of them every day since, even though she hadn't been present at the time.

When it came down to it, Amir knew his brother wasn't guilty of being deceitful or conniving, simply oblivious to the parallels between the young boy and Farah, and why it hurt so much. Fahid was a child whose life had been turned upside down by ill health and the loss of a parent too. It simply didn't seem fair that Amir could turn things around for that family when he couldn't do the same for his own.

Though he'd have to get used to that, he supposed, such was the nature of his job. Treating a child wasn't anything new to him, and, whether the circumstances were close to his daughter's or not, he had a duty of care. Somehow he was going to have to find a way to separate his personal life and feelings from his work.

To be fair to Raed, he was one of the few people who treated Farah the same way he always had, as though he didn't see her wheelchair. Day-to-day life for Amir, however, was a constant reminder of all the things his daughter could no longer do. The only one who knew the struggles they faced on a practical level was Isolde, someone else who never talked down to Farah, or ever saw her as anything other than a capable young girl.

'Isolde! I thought you weren't coming. Djamila said you weren't feeling well.' It was Soraya who alerted him to her arrival and he immediately felt better. If she harboured any resentment for him kissing her, surely she wouldn't have bothered coming to see him before the surgery to wish him luck like all the others.

'I'm a little better so I thought I should come down for support. You said Fahid wouldn't have any family in with him today?' She was avoiding Amir's eye and letting him know he wasn't the reason she was here after all.

His euphoria deflated. 'No, his mother isn't well enough to come down but she signed all the relevant permission papers to give the go-ahead. I said I'd phone her directly once he's out of Theatre.'

This time she had to look at him as she simply said, 'Good.'

'I've told her Fahid won't be able to do any heavy lifting for a while. Can we get the family some support while he recuperates?' Although the surgery should improve the quality of life, post-surgery the young boy still needed time to recover from the operation. Amir wasn't the sort of man who would simply walk away from his patient once his job was done. He might be in the country only temporarily but he still wanted to make sure the young boy would be taken care of in his absence.

'We've been working with his mother to get her to agree to carers coming in throughout the day to help her and relieve Fahid of some of his duties. She's reluctant to let strangers into the house. I think she's afraid social services will accuse her of neglect and take him away from her. Perhaps we could get some volunteers from the centre to call on her in a less formal arrangement to help out.' Efficient Soraya had obviously already taken a great interest in the boy's case. Unsurprising when she probably saw a lot of herself in the child. Her experiences, along with her natural empathy, were qualities that would make a great asset for the royal family.

'I can do it. At least for as long as I'm here. Fahid is probably going to need some physio too to regain his strength post-op so I'm sure we can make arrangements for me to see him here and at home to keep an eye on things.' Isolde surprised them all with her generous offer. Though Amir supposed he should be used to her altruistic tendencies when she'd gone above and beyond the call of duty for him and Farah. He could only hope no one else would take advantage of her kindness the way he had.

'That's a great idea. You and Amir can work together on this one,' Soraya said, looking at him for confirmation.

Unbeknown to her, it did put him and Isolde in a sticky situation, forcing them closer together when he was trying to keep a professional and personal distance from her. But he couldn't deny it would aid Fahid and his family to have them both on his side.

'If that's okay with Isolde?' He tested the waters before committing himself to anything further.

'Sure,' she said flatly, her lack of enthusiasm saying everything she hadn't about the prospect of working together. 'You must let me know what the surgery entails so I can tailor an exercise plan for him.'

'Like any lung surgery it's a major undertaking as the organs are so close to the heart and blood vessels. I'll have to go in through the chest and ribs to remove the lobes, so he'll need a chest drain to remove excess fluid.' It was a standard procedure for him, but all surgery carried risks of complication and treatment post-surgery was equally vital to the patient's recovery and quality of life.

'So, standard physio following that type of operation? Deep-breathing and coughing exercises to help lungs re-expand, and aid breathing?' Isolde was very matter-of-fact. He knew this was as commonplace to her as the surgery was to him but having her on board too gave Fahid a better chance to get his life back on track as soon as possible.

'Yes, and, of course, no heavy lifting for a while to prevent strain on the chest muscles and incision site.'

'Of course. I can start gentle exercises with him in the hospital after the op to get him mobile as soon as possible to help his lung capacity as well as his circulation.'

'That would be great, thank you.'

Amir and Raed might have cleared the air but the tension between him and Isolde was still palpable. Although, despite his faux pas, she was still here in support and planning her part in Fahid's recovery. She could easily have stayed away, or minimised her role in the boy's treatment, but, like him, that simply wasn't in her nature. He admired the dedication to her job, but more than that he admired the woman she was.

Since the kiss he'd tried to put a little distance between them, retiring to bed early in the evenings, and making sure to be in a crowd during the day. It had been for their own benefit, but whenever she looked at him there was an unmistakable wounded look in her eyes and she'd been uncharacteristically subdued since the kiss.

He hadn't wanted to cause an awkward atmosphere between them—if anything, by walking away he'd hoped to avoid just that. What he didn't want was for Isolde to blame herself and believe she'd done something wrong. He'd taken advantage when she'd been at her most vulnerable, confiding in him about her ex and the way he'd manipulated her. Now Amir worried he was guilty of the same thing, kissing her when her defences were at an all-time low.

Despite everything, she was the one he most wanted to see now before going into the operating theatre. He didn't get nervous before surgery but he thought he'd be able to concentrate better knowing things were okay between them. He needed that peace of mind.

'I'm going to go and see Fahid before we go into the surgery. Isolde, perhaps you'd like to walk down with me?' He knew he was playing with fire putting her on the spot this way, but avoiding each other wasn't helping the awkwardness between them.

Isolde contemplated saying no, she wouldn't, but that would only alert Soraya and Raed that something was wrong between them. She'd almost not bothered to come at all today, her conscience getting the better of her at the last minute knowing that little boy was here without any family, probably afraid about what was going to happen to him. They'd only met briefly that day at the centre, but she hoped if he saw a few familiar faces it might give him some comfort. When their parents had been going through their health problems, she and Soraya would've been grateful for friends to support them, and at the end of the day this was what it was all about. Making a difference to a family that were in difficult circumstances, because they didn't want them to struggle the way they had.

When her hesitation over agreeing to accompany Amir began to draw attention from her sister, Isolde gave a hasty, and insincere, 'I'd love to.'

He was the reason it had taken her so long deciding to come after all. That kiss had changed everything between them, and not for the better. It had come out of the blue, but she'd enjoyed it. Lost herself in the moment. She knew she wouldn't have regretted it if he hadn't got up and walked away. Instantly humiliating her, and sullying what had been a beautiful moment. Worse, he'd been avoiding her since, letting her know how sorry he was it had ever happened. It didn't do much for her self-esteem. Especially when she'd laid herself so bare in the moment, shared things with him she'd never told anyone, and left her heart unguarded for a fraction too long.

If she had any self-respect she'd pretend it had never happened too, and carry on as normal instead of being wounded by his subsequent rejection. Or thinking there was a chance they could actually be a couple. When he'd kissed her, all the reasons they shouldn't be together had disappeared. The touch of his lips on hers obliterating all the obstacles she knew they'd have to get over, making them fall away, leaving only her want for him. Without any of the issues that had kept them from moving their friendship on taking up space in her head, she'd had to admit to the attraction and the growing feelings for him. Now he'd made it clear they weren't reciprocated, she didn't know how to put them back in the box and pretend they'd never existed.

'I'm sorry I put you on the spot, but I thought we should talk about what happened between us.' He kept his eyes trained on the corridor before them, not slowing his pace, as if he wanted this resolved before they reached the doors at the bottom. She wasn't so sure it could all be wrapped up in a few seconds. At least not for her.

The way he spoke about the kiss so casually made her cringe at the significance she'd assigned it. 'It's okay. It doesn't matter.'

Suddenly, faced with the possibility of confronting what had happened, and analysing exactly why he wished he'd never kissed her, Isolde wanted to forget the whole business. This time he did stop, glanced around the corridor and pulled her into an empty cubicle, drawing the curtain around for privacy, but making her feel suffocated by her own embarrassment.

'I'm sorry I kissed you.'

'Yeah, well, I gathered that by the way you left me sitting there then proceeded to ignore me for days on end.' She couldn't keep the sarcasm from her voice, her defence mechanism kicking in as he prepared to spell out exactly why he didn't want her.

Amir visibly flinched. 'I know. I handled things badly.'

Isolde snorted. Handling her was what had got them in this mess in the first place.

'I crossed the line and ruined our friendship. If I've been avoiding you it's because I was embarrassed by my behaviour.'

'Wait, what?' Isolde unfolded her arms from her defensive pose as he presented her with a new scenario.

'You were upset and vulnerable and I took advantage of you. I'm sorry. I don't want to lose you from my life, from Farah's life.'

'Amir, I was well aware of what I was doing, what we were doing. I thought… I thought you regretted kissing me. That that was why you walked away.'

A look of relief transformed Amir's face from a frown into a smile. 'I did, but not in the way you think. You were delicate and I believed I'd acted inappropriately. That's why I left, why I've been too embarrassed to face you.'

Isolde laughed, sharing his relief over their crossed wires. 'In case you're in any doubt, I wanted you to kiss me, Amir. I enjoyed it.'

A deep flush infused his cheeks. 'Okay, then I'm glad we got that sorted.'

For a few seconds they stared at each other in silence with stupid grins on their faces, then reality set in.

'But we can't do it again.' It pained her to say it but the fallout from one little kiss had been too great for them to risk happening again when they were going to be tied together for some time with the wedding, Fahid, and Farah. Their circumstances hadn't changed just because they apparently had some chemistry they'd been suppressing all this time. And what a chemistry. She hadn't been able to put that kiss out of her head since it happened and she doubted she ever would.

Amir nodded his head. 'Agreed. Neither of us are in the right place for anything to happen, and I don't want us to spoil what we've got.'

They stared at each other in silence for a moment, as though in mourning for a relationship they could never have. Yet despite their vow to remain platonic there was still that same tension in the air between them, something waiting to snap. Then it did.

In a sudden frenzy of arms and mouths

they were locked in a passionate embrace, kissing harder and with more intensity than the last time their lips had met. Now it was so much more than seeking, and giving, a moment of comfort. A kiss born from that explosion of sexual tension between them, expressing not only that attraction to one another, but feelings they knew they shouldn't be allowing to run amok. And with good reason. This passionate display was intoxicating, all-consuming, and dangerous.

Isolde had been in a relationship before where all common sense went out of the window for the sake of keeping her partner happy. While it was true she was certainly very happy in this very moment, long term she knew it wasn't sustainable. She didn't want to be blinded by her libido. If her past relationship had taught her anything it was that she shouldn't compromise who she was for any man. Amir hadn't tricked her into thinking he was anything but a devoted father so it would be her own fault if she got hurt further down the line when she woke up to the fact he and Farah needed a wife and mother. Roles she'd never wanted and still didn't.

Yet being here in his arms, enveloped in

his warmth, his lips on hers, she'd never felt so wanted. Needed. Loved. It was then she realised she had to put a stop to this before it became a habit they couldn't and didn't want to break.

She pulled away from Amir, dizzy from the kiss and the sudden loss of his attentions. When she looked at him, his eyes almost black with desire as he stumbled back, she could see he was as confused and disoriented by the whole situation as she was. This had caught them both by surprise. When he'd asked her to walk with him, to clear the air, she doubted he'd planned on pulling her into a cubicle and kissing them both senseless. It made it all the more dangerous. He didn't have any more control over his emotions than she did, and if one of them didn't call a halt now they'd both end up in trouble. The last thing she wanted was to wreak havoc in his and Farah's lives and hurt them any more, and that was exactly what would happen if they took this any further.

'That's the last time that can happen,' she said, her pulse still racing, her inner wanton screaming, 'No!' at the top of her voice in protest.

The truth was she wanted it to happen

again and again, obliterating everything else in the world so all she had to think about were Amir's touch and the taste of him on her lips. That was the problem. Every time he kissed her she forgot the reasons why they shouldn't be doing it and just concentrated on enjoying the moment. Forgetting the fundamental problem that he had a daughter, that he was a man she could never simply entertain a fling with when their lives were so deeply entwined, was pain just waiting to happen.

She didn't want to lose him from her life the way she'd lost everyone else she cared about and that was bound to happen when things inevitably didn't work out. They were too different, their plans for the future on opposite paths. That didn't mean she didn't like him, or wasn't hoping for a miracle that it could all somehow work out. Which was exactly why she had to walk away.

If she couldn't be around him without wanting more than a friendship, then she was going to have to wean herself off him. From now on Amir had to be off limits. No more spontaneous passionate embraces, because the euphoria was always going to give way to the ultimate disappointment when the realisation they couldn't take things any further kicked in. She couldn't carry on waiting for this to happen again, hoping some maternal instinct would take over and she'd feel the need to settle down with a family. But in the end she knew Amir and Farah deserved more than her inevitably letting them down.

When Amir didn't make any move to stop her, she knew he'd likely come to the same conclusion.

CHAPTER FIVE

'Okay, team. Let's do this.' Amir rallied everyone in the operating theatre once they knew Fahid was fully under the anaesthetic.

Although, he wasn't feeling as relaxed about the procedure as he'd hoped. Not that he wasn't confident about the surgery—it was something he was very competent and capable in. He had simply hoped that he and Isolde would've cleared the air before he entered the operating theatre. Kissing her again hadn't been in his plans.

Perhaps it was finding out he hadn't crossed the line with her the first time around, that he hadn't misread the situation after all, that had prompted him to do it a second time. It could've been simply that he'd missed her these past days and he'd needed that physical connection to feel whole again. Whatever the reason, he hadn't been able to keep his feelings in check. That overwhelming urge to hold her, to kiss her, to taste her, had consumed him again, and caused him to recklessly act on it.

He wasn't usually the type of person to act on impulse, or in fact to do anything simply because he wanted to. It was in his nature to act appropriately at all times lest he sully the family name, always mulling over the consequences of his actions before he did anything, keeping his reputation as a good son, father, and prince intact. Isolde made him forget all of that, left no time for him to contemplate anything other than his need to have her in his arms. It was his own fault for kissing her in the first place and unleashing all of these feelings, having managed to keep them in check for so long. Now he knew how good it was to kiss her it would be impossible for him to ever erase it from his mind.

It was for the best that it had been Isolde who'd put an end to things because he wasn't sure he would've been capable. When she had come to her senses, he was still lost in the moment and likely would have stayed there for ever if he'd been allowed. Not the actions of a man who was still trying to make it up to his daughter for the last time he'd acted without thinking things through completely. If he'd thought a little more about what a divorce could cost the family and been honest with his wife about how unhappy he was, she would never have driven off with Farah so erratically. He didn't want to make the same mistake again by putting his needs above those of his loved ones.

Farah was more important than any doomed relationship he might hope to pursue with Isolde. He couldn't operate and fix the things preventing her from having a normal life the way he was doing for Fahid, so all he could do was devote himself to making her comfortable. Getting involved with someone she already relied on, a woman who had no desire to be a substitute parent, was not going to improve his daughter's life. If anything, it could make things worse if he took away her ally for his own selfish means.

He looked at Fahid's face, so serene, and totally at his mercy. There was no choice, he supposed, when he was the expert, the one shouldering responsibility for the outcome of this operation.

He made an incision between the boy's ribs and with the aid of a thoracoscope, a small video camera, he was able to remove the lobes. A relatively straightforward procedure for him but one that could change the boy's life dramatically.

It made him think of Farah, the way she relied on him to simply get her through life. Despite all the ways he'd let her down so far.

Amir desperately needed to be the same steady rock for his daughter as he was for this little boy relying on him to make his life better. That wasn't going to happen when he still had eyes on Isolde. It was time for him to back away, to take control of his life the way he did in the operating theatre. Once the wedding was over he needed to get back to a more professional relationship with Isolde. One where Farah's feelings and development were more important than theirs. In the meantime, they had Fahid and the wedding to keep them distracted. Hopefully.

'I know we don't have any of our fancy hospital equipment out here, Farah, but we still need to keep your body strong to maintain what movement you do have.' Isolde had managed to avoid Amir for less than twenty four hours since she had to keep up with Farah's physiotherapy, but at least he'd given them some space today. Putting their personal issues aside so she could focus on her patient.

They had to keep up the strengthening exercises at least so the progress Farah had made so far wouldn't be in vain. With some weight training and aerobic exercises she had at least been able to recover upper-body movement. It was a lot to ask of the young girl every day but to her credit she worked hard, so determined was she to walk again.

'Do you think I could dance at the wedding?' she asked tentatively.

Isolde didn't want to disappoint her but she wanted to be realistic about the chances of that happening. 'Well, you're very adept at your wheelchair now. I think you'll be able to spin and twirl like everyone else on the dance floor.'

'You know what I mean.' Farah watched her through narrowed eyes.

'You won't be able to do anything if you don't do these exercises...'

Farah sighed, but continued with the seated ankle exercises, raising her toes up towards the calf muscles, then relaxing. These days she was able to do more without Isolde's assistance but there was still a long way to go for complete independence of mobility.

She moved on to the marching exercises, starting with both feet on the ground, then lifting up alternate knees. The movement mimicked a walking motion without causing pressure to the joints. Spinal cord injury exercises stimulated the undamaged regions of the spinal cord as well as strengthening the pathways that controlled movement, which was why it was important to stick to the routine.

'Can I try the treadmill?' Farah asked once she'd completed the reps.

'We don't have the harness to support your body weight. I'm not sure it would be such a good idea.' Isolde didn't want any injuries to set back her recovery or upset Amir.

'Can't I try? I'll be careful. I promise.'

Isolde knew it was the one time Farah felt as though she were actually walking again and she didn't want to do anything that might upset her. 'I suppose we could keep it on the lowest setting and I could walk behind you.'

The little girl's smile was the incentive to make it work. Even if they only managed a couple of steps she knew it would please Farah and give her a sense of achievement. If she stumbled at all Isolde would switch off the machine.

She helped Farah out of her chair, grateful that the arm exercises had given the girl the strength to support her body weight on the hand rails. Isolde positioned herself directly behind Farah, hoping they wouldn't both end up in a heap on the floor. She turned on the treadmill and made sure it was at the lowest, slowest setting. For the first few steps she nudged the backs of Farah's knees with hers to promote the walking movement but in no time at all Farah managed to do it on her own.

'I'm doing it!' she cried out, the excitement and effort present in every trembling limb.

'You're amazing, Farah.' She was a truly remarkable little girl who'd put in more work than a lot of Isolde's older patients to achieve these spectacular results.

When she could see Farah starting to tire, her shaky steps not quite keeping pace with the machine, she decided to call it a day.

'I'm going to turn the treadmill off now, Farah, okay. We can do some more tomorrow.'

When Farah didn't argue she knew this new milestone had taken an extra effort. Isolde took her time transferring her back into her wheelchair even though she was bubbling with excitement.

'I can't wait to tell your father. He's going to be so proud.' She could only imagine how happy it would make Amir to see his little girl walk again. Even though it was baby steps at the moment, it augured well for the future. She knew all he wanted was for his daughter to be happy again, and hopefully it would alleviate some of that unnecessary guilt he was carrying.

Although things between them were complicated, Isolde still cared about Amir, and wanted only the best for him and his daughter. The lapses of judgement that kept finding them falling onto one another's mouths was an inconvenience, a consequence of spending so much time with someone she admired so greatly. They really needed to be careful before one, or both, of them got hurt. It wasn't as though they were young, free and single to carry on how they liked. They had complications and weighty baggage, which made anything long term impossible. For now, however, they had to maintain a united front for the family's sake and she wasn't sure how keeping secrets would impact on their already unstable relationship.

'Can't we keep it a secret? I want to surprise him at the wedding.'

'I don't know, Farah, it doesn't seem right to keep this from him.'

Isolde could see why she would want to surprise him but she wasn't comfortable with the idea of keeping secrets from Amir when it came to his daughter. He was fiercely protective and invested in Farah's recovery and he might see it as a betrayal of trust for her physiotherapist to keep this information from him. There was also the manner in which Farah intended to reveal the news to him. Doing it in a very public environment added extra pressure on her to replicate those few precious independent steps and Isolde didn't want the little girl to end up embarrassed or hurt if things didn't go to plan. Certainly that was something Amir would never forgive her for.

'Please, Isolde.' Those familiar big brown eyes, so much like her father's, were able to persuade Isolde to do anything.

That was how she knew she was in so much mess already.

'I need you to cough for me, Fahid. If we can't keep your airways clear it can lead to infection,' Isolde told the boy, trying once more to coax him into his exercises. He'd been cooperative at the hospital but now, four days later, he was home, and a little more resistant.

'It hurts…'

'Now, Fahid, you know Isolde and I only want you to get better. If you do these exercises now, you'll be back on your feet in no time. It's all to help you breathe easier so you can be active for longer periods of time.' Amir sat down beside him on the sofa so he was at eye level, speaking to the boy as a friend rather than his surgeon or an authoritative adult figure. He had a way with children, and all of his patients. Isolde too at times.

He made it seem as though they were very much a team when they were working together in situations like this. Often her job could be isolating, when she worked independently from the doctors and nurses. Of course she had to liaise with medical teams to get an overall view of a patient's treatment, and sometimes it took another colleague to help her with certain patients, but mostly she worked alone. It was nice to have someone to play off against to get a patient's co-operation, and to get a clearer picture of a patient's journey.

She usually focused on the aftercare, but having Amir to explain what Fahid had gone through in surgery gave her a greater insight into what he'd gone through thus far. As well as reminding her of the incredible job Amir did on a daily basis. Carrying out major surgery on such a young patient should not be something taken for granted and it was only treated as unremarkable because of the effortless, efficient way Amir carried out these life-enhancing, sometimes life-saving procedures.

Since Olly, she'd strived for a greater independence, afraid of anyone else trying to change who she was. Even living with Soraya had been challenging at times, regardless that her sister had cooked and cleaned for her like old times. She'd got used to being on her own, and she'd had to once Soraya had moved to Zaki. Now she was beginning to see the benefits of having someone else around.

Amir never tried to take over, only ever to assist, to try and make things easier for her. He didn't attempt to change her or threaten her independence. Instead, he showed her what a difference a supportive partner could make. Even if it was only in a professional capacity.

Perhaps some day she would even venture to share her personal life with someone again if they could show the same kind of respect for her that Amir did. It was a shame being with him in particular would mean compromising who she was and what she wanted all over again.

'Okay, Fahid, I want you to take a big deep breath slowly in through your nose. Hold for two seconds then breath slowly out through your mouth. We're going to repeat this five times.' Isolde coached him through his breathing exercises, working towards strengthening his lungs to get them functioning at full capacity again.

'It won't be long before you're playing football again,' Amir added, making the boy's smile wider than ever and persuading him it was in his best interests to co-operate.

They'd decided, in order to make him more comfortable, they'd do their follow-up visits at home, where his mother could be present, and his surroundings would be less intimidating. It was best for Fahid and his mother, but awkward for her and Amir given their current circumstances.

After yet another lapse into forbidden territory—Amir's lips—she should have been trying harder than ever to keep her distance from him, but now they simply had more reason to be spending time together. As though fate were conspiring to torture her by repeatedly pushing him into her eyeline.

He looked good today, as always. When visiting Fahid he kept it casual—no tie, shirt collar open and sleeves rolled up over his thick forearms. Total Isolde bait. She supposed it was an attempt to be more laid-back around their young patient, less formal, and therefore less intimidating. Everything Amir did was calculated to maximise the benefit towards others. That was why those spontaneous passionate clinches they kept falling into seemed so out of character for him.

She confessed, the idea that she could inspire such impulsive behaviour in him did little to quell her ardent admiration for him. There was something inherently sexy in making a man lose control like that in his pursuit of her. It was reciprocated, of course, but she had been known in the past for her reckless tendencies. Amir, on the other hand, had apparently lived the life of a saint. His only crime, according to him, was failing to make his marriage work. That made her feel like a wanton hussy, seducing him away from his life of order and best behaviour. Except she hadn't encouraged anything until he'd kissed her. Then all bets were off. How was she supposed to have resisted such undisguised lust from a man she'd apparently been harbouring a secret crush on for the best part of the year?

She didn't know when she'd crossed that line from respecting him at work, admiring his devotion to his daughter, and enjoying his company, to wanting him to kiss her as if they'd just hooked up in the alley behind a dive bar. But it was apparent there was no going back.

Despite their best intentions, trying to remain emotionally and physically distant, except when treating Fahid, it wasn't going to erase the memories or the feelings she had towards him. She hadn't said anything yet through fear of upsetting anyone before the wedding, but she might have to pass Farah's care on to someone else when they got back home. The last thing she wanted to do was upset the little girl, or set back her recovery in any way. However, she wanted the best for her, and that might have to be a different physiotherapist. One who wouldn't be mooning over her father.

The journey here hadn't been the most comfortable, despite the luxury car they'd travelled in. Making small talk, trying to keep to the safe topic of their mutual patient, had been stilted and unnatural. Mostly because there was so much other, personal stuff they had apparently decided they didn't need to discuss. Those kisses, the unresolved feelings they clearly had for one another, hung in the air between them. That crackling electricity making it a real possibility that they could suddenly launch themselves at one another at any given moment for a repeat performance. Perhaps that was why he'd squeezed himself into the furthest corner of the car away from her.

It was this kind of behaviour, this tension, that made working together long term completely untenable.

'Thanks again for doing this. I feel like a lottery winner having members of the royal family coming into my home to tend to my boy.' Fahid's mother had been effusive with her gratitude from the moment they'd walked in the door. This was partially for her benefit too so she would feel as though she was involved with her son's treatment and wasn't completely powerless as it all happened around her. Isolde knew something about that. From the moment her parents had died she didn't think she'd had much of a say in anything. It had taken until that make-or-break talk with Olly for her to finally stand up and speak her mind, assert her autonomy over her own body, and life, by telling him she didn't want children under any circumstances.

She was sure when Fahid's mother had decided to have a family she hadn't expected it to be this way. There'd been no plan for his father to die and leave her as a single parent, or for her own health problems to impact on her son's life. This was exactly what Isolde wanted to avoid—somehow ending up causing her child the pain she and Soraya had gone through during their childhood. She was making sure she wasn't going to be responsible for inflicting this sort of pain.

It was obvious this woman loved her son, that he was her life. There were happy, smiling photographs of the pair all over the flat, and his toys littered the floor. But it was also apparent that he had the weight of responsibility that no child his age should have to endure. In her haste to welcome Isolde and Amir, Fahid's mother had directed him to make tea, offer them food, and tidy up to make room for them. All of which they'd protested against, of course. This was his life, but it shouldn't have to be.

'Not at all. We're here in our professional capacity,' Amir reminded her, probably trying to avoid the usual bowing and scraping that went on any time he met a member of the public, who all seemed as enamoured with him as Isolde. Almost.

'And strictly speaking I'm not a member of the royal family so there's definitely no need to stand on ceremony for me,' Isolde added.

'Thank you all the same,' Fahid's mother insisted. 'I don't know where I'd be without Fahid.' Her voice wobbled with emotion and Isolde considered how much the woman must've fretted over her son's health problems and the effect it could have had on both of them. He was her lifeline and her link to the outside world. All of the mobility aids dotted around, and the fact she hadn't come to the door to greet them, suggested her movements were limited. Hopefully now Fahid had gone through his surgery and they were working on his recovery, he would find an improvement in his quality of life that would filter through to his mother too.

'My sister said she was trying to get some help for you at home. Have you had anyone contact you?' It was another way of relieving Fahid's burden at home and Isolde knew Soraya was keen to give him the sort of childhood she'd been denied because of her duty to family. If it came to it, Isolde wouldn't be surprised if her sister came out and cooked and cleaned for the family if it meant Fahid had more chance to go out and play, and just be a little boy.

'Yes. We're going to have someone coming out several times a day to help me around the house and cook us some dinner. It's going to make such a difference to both of us.' The gratitude and optimism over the change was apparent in Fahid's mother's smile, and it made Isolde suddenly well up.

It was emotional for Isolde knowing that they'd been able to bring some positive changes to help this little family, and she knew that was all Soraya wanted too.

'I'll let Soraya know. She was very keen to get everyone involved to help you both, as was Raed.' She thought of the initial introduction they'd had to Fahid and the impact it had on Amir. It was bound to be on his mind every time he followed up on Fahid's progress that his own daughter hadn't been so fortunate, that her problems couldn't be solved with a few phone calls and favours. If all she'd needed was a dedicated surgeon and someone who cared she would have been cured a long time ago.

Isolde had been continuing in private with Farah's exercises since they'd flown out while Amir had been dealing with family matters and Fahid. Isolde's first instinct had been to run and fetch Amir to witness that first breakthrough, knowing it was everything he'd been striving for, but Farah had asked her not to. Her continued progress made it harder not to share the news with him.

She got the impression the little girl was afraid to get her father's hopes up in case it didn't happen again. Neither of them had wanted to put her under pressure to 'perform', especially with the wedding coming up. There was the possibility that the 'establishment', the PR managers behind the scenes concerned with the family's appearance, might prefer if she ditched the wheelchair for aesthetic reasons if she could, but it wouldn't have been fair to expect so much from her during such a spectacle. Instead, they had continued working on those first baby steps in private. Today Farah had managed a stilted walk a little farther and both of them had been fit to burst from the excitement.

It felt wrong not to share such a huge development with Amir, but she had to put Farah's needs first. Strictly speaking she wasn't on the work clock so she didn't think it would pose a risk to her job by keeping the information from him. Although there was a moral question. She could only hope things worked out the way Farah wanted and he would be so happy he'd forgive Isolde for her part in the deceit.

'Everything seems to be healing as it should. We'll keep an eye on Fahid while we're in the country, but when we head back to the UK we'll have to hand over his care to another team. Don't worry though, they'll be under strict orders from the royal family to look after him,' Amir joked after he'd finished his examination of Fahid.

Both he and Isolde made their move to leave.

'We'll see ourselves out. Don't get up. It was very nice to meet you.' Isolde shook hands with the woman and Amir followed.

'Thank you for everything. We're so privileged to have had your help this far, and thank your family for all they've done for us. You have no idea how much it means to us.' Fahid's mother shuffled to the edge of the sofa and grabbed them both into a hug.

Isolde knew all too well how much their assistance had changed the lives of this family. It had given them some independence, and hopefully Fahid would get to have more of a childhood. Everything she wished someone had given to her sister when they were younger. Still, she couldn't change history and making a difference to someone else's life was the next best thing.

Once they'd said their goodbyes, she and Amir got back into the car. She slumped onto the back seat and closed her eyes, emotionally drained by the visit.

'Are you okay?'

The sound of Amir's voice filled the back of the car and filtered through the fog in Isolde's head.

'I'm not the one who's just gone through major surgery, or who struggles to do anything without physical help.'

Okay, so she was a little tetchy as they walked away knowing it was probably the last time she'd see them again, their problems no longer hers to worry about. She didn't feel good about walking away even though Fahid and his mother seemed happy enough with the way things had gone. As though her conscience should be salved now she'd done her bit and they were no longer her concern.

How many times had Soraya had visits from do-gooders who'd promised the world only for them never to be heard of again? Too many to mention. She didn't want to be one of those fake people, but there was nothing she could do about it unless she prolonged her stay in the country. Something that would not go down well with her boss or her landlord. The only thing she could do was ask Soraya to keep her up to date on their progress and offer virtual assistance from afar if needed.

'I know, but it's clear it had an effect on you.' Amir spoke softly, gently, as though he were talking to an easily spooked horse, trying to tame her before she lashed out again.

It wasn't his fault that she couldn't handle being reminded of the bad old days left to Soraya to fend for them when their parents had gone, or the fact she had to go home. These past few days feeling as though she had her family back, of being part of something, had been great. She wasn't looking forward to returning home alone.

'Yes, well, I'm a big girl. I'll get over it.' She had to or she'd end up bitter and twisted, resenting the fact that she couldn't do more for others, or make things work with him.

'It's just…working with Fahid is bringing up a lot of emotional issues for both of us. You were there for me when I had my wobble.' He gave her a coy smile that said he was embarrassed over the whole affair, his emotional outburst at the centre that day having been the catalyst for all the subsequent trouble between them. 'I just want you to know I'm here if you need to talk.'

'Thanks, but I'll be okay,' she said, and forced her face to reverse the frown etched on her forehead so he wouldn't think there was anything wrong.

If there was one thing she didn't need right now it was Amir being nice to her, being sympathetic and showing an understanding of the issues from her past that she was only just coming to terms with herself.

It was becoming clear that the more she was around him, the more reasons she had to like him, which in these circumstances wasn't a good thing. This wedding couldn't come soon enough so she could do her duty as Soraya's sister, celebrate her nuptials, then get the hell out of Amir's orbit before things got completely out of control.

CHAPTER SIX

'NERVOUS?'

'A bit. Although I'm not sure I'm the one who's supposed to need reassurance today. You have to be the most laid-back bride I've ever seen, Soraya. No one would ever guess you're about to marry into the royal family before the eyes of the world. Are you on drugs?'

Soraya laughed. 'No drugs. I'm just happy to be marrying the love of my life.'

Isolde couldn't believe her sister was this relaxed on her wedding day without some sort of sedative to keep her from flailing around. Worked up about appearing in public, Isolde had already had a breakdown over her wayward locks and smudged mascara, and she was only background crew. Her anxiety over the forthcoming day had caused her stomach to roll so much she hadn't been able to touch the champagne breakfast that had been laid out for them this morning, and she was only the bridesmaid.

Mind you, she had a lot on her mind. Including the prospect of spending the day in Amir's company, something they'd both learned wasn't a good idea these days. Left unsupervised they tended to get a bit carried away. Perhaps it was a blessing in disguise they'd be surrounded by photographers and film crews for most of the day. Hopefully it should remove that temptation of throwing themselves at one another if there was a danger of someone catching it on camera. They'd have some explaining to do to a lot of people if they were caught in a compromising position.

There was also the matter of Farah's planned surprise. Although it was scheduled to happen during the evening reception, which would be held for family and friends only, away from the press, there was a lot at stake. She didn't want anyone to be embarrassed or disappointed if things didn't work out the way they hoped, especially Amir and Farah. Nor did she want Amir to be mad at her for keeping his daughter's secret. There was a separate anxiety swirling around her body at how

Amir was going to react and if she was going to be in the firing line. Given that he was a senior member of the royal family, there was a real possibility she'd committed some sort of treason, and a firing squad might be seen as just punishment for a Jezebel who kept kissing the widowed Prince and was now interfering in family matters.

'I'm so happy for you, sis. You look beautiful.' That happiness she spoke of was radiating out of her every pore, her love for Raed shining brightly on her face.

'Well, I did have a team of stylists.' Soraya screwed up her nose, batting away any compliments, but she couldn't convince Isolde she was anything but stunning today.

Her ivory silk dress clung beautifully to her curves, though preserved her modesty with the lace collar and sleeves. She was every inch the fairy-tale princess.

'We had the same team and I do not even compare. I think I have so many pins in my hair trying to keep it in place they're embedded in my scalp, and I think you mistakenly assigned me a make-up artist who usually works on drag queens.'

They were standing in front of the huge crystal-encrusted mirror in the suite the hotel had given them to get ready in. The team who had brushed and primped and squeezed them into submission had gone now so Isolde assumed it was safe to assert some damage control.

She took a tissue and began to wipe carefully at the heavy dark eye make-up and blusher staining her pale complexion. It was too much, too bold, for someone who usually got by with some lip gloss and face powder.

Soraya gave her a gentle push. 'It's not that bad, but you don't need it.'

She took the tissue and dabbed it on her tongue to wipe away the excess eyeliner, making Isolde grin.

'What's so funny?' Soraya demanded to know.

'This. It's just like being a kid again when I came in covered in dirt from playing outside and you'd take a handkerchief and scrub my face with it.'

Not all the memories of growing up were bad but they tended to fade into the background against the struggles they'd faced. Soraya had been her mother, father and grandmother figure all rolled into one. The one who'd cleaned her up, mopped her tears and baked for her. Doing all she could to give

Isolde as normal a childhood as possible despite their circumstances.

Soraya's smile was a little wobbly. 'We did it, didn't we? Despite everything, we made it through. Who would've thought we'd end up hobnobbing with royalty? I'm proud of you, Isolde, for everything you've become, helping Farah and Fahid. Thank you for being my sister.'

All the emotion Isolde had been trying to hold at bay today was suddenly rushing up to meet Soraya's outpouring, and she gulped in an attempt to keep it away for a little longer.

'Don't start crying! You'll set me off, and we don't want to be walking down that aisle looking like two demented pandas. Raed will run a mile.' Isolde managed to turn Soraya's sentimental sob into a hiccup-laugh.

She cleared her throat and dabbed her eyes. 'You're right. The tears can wait until you have to go home and I'm forced to say goodbye to you.'

Isolde didn't want to think about that. It wasn't going to help stem this tidal wave of sorrow and loss threatening to drown her when she thought how long it might be before she saw her sister again. Of course, there would be visits and family celebrations, but it was never going to be just the two of them again. As selfish as it sounded, and as happy as she was that her sister had found her soulmate, she couldn't help think about where it left her, without her sister to guide her and keep her out of trouble.

'Hey, it's not goodbye, it's *au revoir* for now,' Isolde managed to say through the unshed tears, trying to lighten the mood with some cheese.

'You're such a dork sometimes.' Soraya sniffed through a laugh, but Isolde had successfully helped to avoid another make-up catastrophe.

'Yes, but people love me for it. Now, where is the remaining member of our little girl band?' She and Soraya had got ready together. It had given them some much-needed sister time, which there hadn't been a lot of recently. There wasn't a lot of opportunity for the two of them to be on their own when there was so much going on at the palace, and this made today even more special.

'Farah's with Djamila getting ready. She should be here any minute. I assume Raed and Amir are having their heart-to-heart talk too. I know he's not looking forward to saying goodbye either.' Soraya slipped into her matching ivory silk heels and stood in front of the mirror again as she put her earrings in.

'Yes, I know Amir is missing his family, as is Farah. Wait, I've got something for you.' Isolde rushed off to grab the tatty blue velvet box from her bag, which she'd brought from home, and presented it to her sister.

'Mum's necklace?' Soraya traced her fingers over the pearl necklace nestled in the silky lining.

'You don't have to wear it, but I thought it could be your something borrowed.' They didn't have a lot of keepsakes from their parents. For as long as she could remember they'd been ill, unable to work, with little money coming in to buy nice things. Though they'd always found money for their cigarettes. The necklace had always been precious to Isolde. Despite being the eldest, Soraya had passed it on to her when their mother had died. A selfless gesture she was forever grateful for when it gave her something tangible of her mother. A memory other than sickness. She remembered her mother wearing it, seeing it nestled around her neck when she bent down to kiss Isolde at night. At least now Isolde was able to give a little piece of their mother back on this special occasion.

'Thank you,' Soraya said as she fastened the pearls around her neck. 'It will feel like I have Mum with me today in some small way.'

Sometimes Isolde forgot how much of an impact their parents' death had had on her older sister beyond the financial difficulties it had left. Isolde had been too young to really comprehend what had happened at the time, and had simply substituted Soraya into that parenting role, even though she'd been barely an adult at eighteen, too young to parent another child. In hindsight it was Soraya who'd perhaps suffered the greater loss, and had to set her grief aside to look after her sibling. Lending her their mother's necklace on her wedding day was the least she could do.

Isolde gave her a hug, careful not to crease her beautiful dress before she made her grand entrance.

'I wish you could stay,' Soraya said on a sigh. 'I mean long term. Amir and Farah too.'

'And give up my amazing flat? Impossible.' Although she wasn't being serious, the dream remained out of reach. As much as she wished they could be one big happy family living the life of luxury out here, it wasn't going to happen. Her time out here had told Isolde one thing and that was she needed to put more distance between her and Amir, not entangle their lives even further.

'Is there something going on with you and Amir?' As always Soraya seemed to see right through her, but this wasn't the time to get into the latest mess she'd got herself into. Even Super Sis couldn't get her out of this one and it wasn't fair to even involve her now, when she should be focusing on getting married. This was her wedding day, not another 'Isolde screws up and I have to fix it' day. They'd both grown up and finally cut those apron strings and it wouldn't be fair to either of them to try and reattach them now.

So she lied.

'No. Not at all. I've just been spending a lot of time at his place getting Farah's input with these dresses. I think the girl really has a future in fashion, you know.' She tried to change the subject but she could see by Soraya's face she wasn't buying it, or willing to move on.

'It's just…there's a bit of an atmosphere between you. Raed's noticed it too. You seemed so relaxed in each other's company at that afternoon tea we had in the hotel, and now… I don't know, it's as if you can't stand to be in the same room as one another now.'

Isolde shrugged. 'You know me, I always outstay my welcome. Perhaps he got fed up with me coming around so often. It doesn't matter now, does it? The dresses are finished so I won't have to go round to his any more.'

'Hmm… Well, whatever it is, I hope it's not influencing your decision not to move out here. You know I'd love to have you stay.'

'Hey, there's only room for one princess in this family and that's you. Now, I think we've kept your husband-to-be waiting long enough. Let's go get your gorgeous flower girl and roll.'

The only thing rolling was Soraya's eyes. 'Just so you know, we're not done with this. I have the small matter of marrying the Crown Prince to take care of, but believe me, Isolde Yarrow, I will get to the bottom of whatever is going on with you.'

'Yes, ma'am.' Isolde gave her a mock salute, treating her promise lightly.

During their childhood Isolde had folded easily under Soraya's interrogation, and always ended up spilling her guts, forced to face the consequences. She suspected the same would be true now, even though they weren't talking about a broken ornament or some stolen sweets she had to confess to.

This was about her feelings for Amir, something she wasn't ready to face up to herself yet. The prospect of doing so, and with her sister, should have been terrifying, but Isolde remained relatively calm. Because once the ceremony was over she was going home and leaving the whole royal family behind her. It was the only way to survive.

Amir's hands were sweaty, he was swaying on his feet, and his heart was pounding. Yet he wasn't even the one getting married. He'd been through this before and hadn't felt this nervous. His wedding had been every bit as grand and well attended, with almost the same press interest, but he'd felt in control then. With a life mapped out before him, marrying the right woman and securing his rightful place in the royal family. It was all a lie of course, but he hadn't realised at the time it was all part of trying to be the perfect son and prince. Now he had no idea what the future held for him or Farah.

If anything this past year had helped him understand why Raed had planned to abandon his position once upon a time. It was too much pressure. Especially now he had Farah to think about. There was nothing more important to him than her welfare. That was why he hadn't pursued Isolde any further when she'd pushed him away, even though he'd wanted to. He knew spending time with Fahid was difficult, it was for him too for different reasons. All he'd done was try and reach out to her, to offer some support, but it was clear she didn't want anything to do with him any more. It was probably for the best when anything more between them than Farah's welfare would be sure to end in tears.

'Are they coming yet?' Raed whispered to him, his eyes trained firmly on the front of the church, showing great restraint.

Amir cast a glance over his shoulder as the organ began to play. 'They're beautiful.'

Soraya looked stunning as she made her way towards them, her veil coyly covering her face, her body sheathed in silk. But it was her bridesmaids who'd captured his attention first. Isolde was pushing Farah's wheelchair, which had been wrapped in ribbon and flowers, both wearing full-length pale green dresses that perfectly matched the colour of his tunic. It was the first time he'd been allowed to see what they'd been working so hard on and he was astounded by what they'd produced.

The pair had enjoyed keeping their secrets, giggling and whispering on those evenings when Isolde had come over and shared dinner with them. The only clues he'd garnered were the fabric samples he'd found on occasion, offcuts from where Isolde had altered the dresses after one of their fittings. The surprise was worth the wait. They both looked incredible, and so happy. He knew Farah wanted to keep her legs covered to hide the scars she'd been left with since the accident, but Isolde had opted to wear the same design, probably so she wouldn't feel self-conscious. If he'd thought he wouldn't make a spectacle of himself he'd have run over and hugged them both, he was so proud. Instead, all he could do was smile as they came to stand across the aisle from him and Raed. Isolde smiled back at him.

You look fabulous, he mouthed, managing to refrain from giving a chef's kiss and completely embarrassing everyone in public.

Thank you, she mouthed back, giving a little curtsey.

Seeing Farah so happy, and with the knowledge Isolde hadn't requested a personal exclusion zone so he couldn't be within a hundred feet of her, he was able to relax a little bit.

He preferred it when they were able to joke around with one another rather than getting upset and finding excuses to stay away from one another. Sometimes he almost wished they could go back to the time before they'd realised they liked kissing one another.

Soraya turned and handed her bouquet to Isolde, then faced Raed, who lifted her veil. When his brother saw his bride properly for the first time, Amir could see he was about to lose it. He knew the feeling, but he was also aware that the eyes of the world were upon them. Amir placed a hand at his brother's back, silently urging him to hold it together. Raed straightened up, cleared his throat, and Amir hoped the moment had passed for both of them as the ceremony began.

He listened along with the rest of the people there as Raed and Soraya said their vows. It was only when they reached the 'Till death do us part', bit that he got a tad overwhelmed. Those feelings of guilt and regret that always tended to show up when he thought of the accident, and the way his marriage had come to a traumatic end, made him think of his own vows. He'd meant every word when he'd said them, but he didn't think he'd married for the right reasons. Certainly, he didn't remember looking at his wife the way Raed looked at Soraya, as if his whole life depended on being with her.

He felt more like that about Isolde than he ever had about his wife, which was what made the whole situation so difficult. Farah was so fond of her, and she'd done so much to help his daughter rediscover her confidence, he didn't want to lose her, but he also knew that it would be painful to be around her every day knowing they couldn't be together. Isolde was most definitely not the right woman for him, but she was the one he still wanted. As always he'd do whatever was right for his daughter and today he'd simply have to set his own needs aside and enjoy the day. It might be the last time they were all together and it was a celebration of his brother finding his soul mate. Something that didn't always work out for everyone else.

'Doesn't Papa look handsome today?' Farah broke the silence in the car only to make things even more awkward.

Yes, Amir looked handsome enough in his silk tunic and trousers that she could certainly have wished away the entire congregation and dragged him into the cloisters for a snog, but she certainly couldn't say that. Not to Farah, nor her father, if they were all to get through this day unscathed.

'No one is looking at me when they have such beautiful dresses to admire. You both look wonderful and I'm so proud of you.' Amir reached across the back seat to hug his daughter, thus successfully changing the subject so Isolde could avoid being put on the spot.

Isolde thought he deserved to be told how pretty he looked today too. 'Yes, your papa is very handsome, Farah. I'm sure there will be a queue of ladies waiting to add him to their dance card tonight.'

The thought of it made her queasy. Poor, hot widower Amir was having the spotlight shone on him today and she had no doubt it would earn him a new team of admirers who would willingly throw themselves at him in the hope of catching his attention. She'd done it herself on occasion, which was why she'd been using Farah as a barrier between them all day, emotionally and physically. Given their positions in the wedding, spending time together today had been inevitable, but at least they'd had Farah to fuss over and keep them from focusing on the lingering glances they kept throwing one another.

It had been a big day for all of them already with the televised ceremony, the official photographs and the reception. Now they were on their way to the evening reception back at the palace where they could let their hair down away from prying eyes and the pressure to be on their best behaviour would finally be off.

Although she could quite happily just crawl into bed and bypass it altogether she was so exhausted. Perhaps she could sneak off after the happy couple had their first dance. Soraya and Raed were so wrapped up in each other she doubted she'd be missed anyway. Not that she begrudged either of them the joy they'd clearly found in one another when life hadn't been easy up until now, especially for Soraya. However, she'd be lying if she said there wasn't a green-eyed monster waiting in the wings watching them declare their love for one another and wishing for the impossible, wishing someone could love her unconditionally too. Where not wanting to traumatise another generation would be respected, not seen as a fatal flaw in a relationship.

'I'm afraid I'll be booked up all night with

my favourite girl.' He hugged Farah a little tighter and went some way to taming Isolde's wild jealousy. Perhaps she wouldn't have to resist a catfight on the dance floor after all.

'I don't mind if you want to dance with Isolde, Papa.' Farah's generous offer to share her father with Isolde was touching, but it also raised more red flags. As if they needed any more.

'That's okay, Farah. I'm not much of a dancer. I wouldn't want to embarrass your dad.' Nor would she want anyone to get the wrong impression. Soraya was already suspicious something was going on and she was sure the two of them slow-dancing would give away just how close they'd become. She was sure she wasn't a good enough actress to pretend being in Amir's arms wasn't exactly where she wanted to be.

'Papa wouldn't be embarrassed, would you, Papa?' There was something in the way Farah looked up at her father, as though she was desperate for the two of them to be together, that really set alarm bells ringing for Isolde.

Amir glanced at her over the top of his daughter's head, a frown deepening across his forehead. He clearly didn't know what had brought this on either. 'Of course I wouldn't be embarrassed to dance with Isolde but we don't force anyone to do anything they're not comfortable with, do we, sweetheart?'

'Yes, but I know Isolde wants to dance with you, so that's okay.' Farah sat back in her seat, arms folded, very confident in her belief.

Isolde saw her worried expression reflected in Amir's face, both of them clearly wondering how she'd come to that conclusion. Whether Isolde had inadvertently said or done something to indicate that, or Farah had decided she wanted to push them together, it was a concerning development. It felt as though Farah was trying to matchmake between them, and Isolde didn't want to break her heart along with her own when she had to go home and leave them behind. Although it was flattering that the little girl saw her as a romantic interest for her father, it wouldn't do to let her get carried away by the notion.

Things were difficult enough between Isolde and Amir, trying to dodge their own feelings because of the repercussions their actions could have, without figuring Farah's feelings into the equation too. Neither of them would ever dream of hurting her, and that was exactly the reason they'd tried to keep what had happened between them under wraps.

Isolde had even kept the details of their kisses from Soraya though she was fit to burst with the secret, dying to share with someone about how much she'd enjoyed every second. All in vain apparently, if Farah had picked up on the tension between them. They hadn't been as discreet as they'd assumed if everyone around them could sense something was amiss. All the more reason to get some distance between them quick. Once they were back to their own lives, away from the glare of publicity and watchful family members, hopefully all interest in their private feelings would die down. Even if the actual emotions involved might take longer to dissipate, if at all.

They let the matter drop rather than fuel whatever fantasy Farah was harbouring. Isolde prayed that the surprise Farah had in store for her father would take her mind off anything else. If all went to plan everyone would be distracted and maybe that would even be the time for Isolde to slip away undetected.

Suddenly the sound of screeching brakes filled the air and the car lurched forward, pushing all three of them violently forward. Then they were spinning. Isolde grabbed hold of the edge of her seat with one hand, and Farah with the other. Amir too was doing his best to shield her, one arm stretched out across her, trying to keep her back in her seat.

The spinning and the squealing of tyres trying to get purchase on the tarmac seemed to last an eternity, but it was probably only seconds before the car came to a shuddering standstill.

'Are you two okay?' Amir's concern for them both was immediate.

'I'm fine. Farah, are you hurt?' Isolde gave her a brief check over and, while there were no obvious injuries, the little girl was sobbing hard.

Amir undid her seat belt and gathered her up into his arms. 'Shh, sweetheart. Everyone's all right.'

It was then Isolde realised the trauma this must be bringing back to the little girl after the accident that had cost her her mobility and her mother. 'I'll go and see what happened but we're all okay, Farah.'

Amir looked as though he was going to stop her then thought better of it, simply nodding as she tried to get her door open. It took brute force and a shoulder-bump to finally wrench it ajar wide enough to try and shimmy out. The vehicle was wedged up against a tree, the car door taking the brunt of the impact. She managed to wriggle the top half of her body out of the gap and planted her hands on the car roof to lever the rest of her body out. The fabric of her dress ripped as she forced her hips through the gap, and she winced as the jagged metal where the door had been damaged grazed along her skin.

'Isolde, are you okay? Do you need me to come out?' Amir asked, apparently having witnessed her minor injury.

'No. I'm fine. You stay with Farah until I can get some help,' she said through gritted teeth, willing the sharp pain away.

Given the occasion, and the people involved, she was sure it wouldn't be long before help arrived, even though they were out in the country. They'd been in a convoy of cars following the royal carriage containing Soraya and Raed. Quite the spectacle. Whatever had caused the accident she was sure it wouldn't go unnoticed. Especially when they were due at the palace.

Once she managed to squeeze herself free, collapsing in a heap on the grass verge in a very undignified manner, she was able to see something of what had occurred. A motorcycle belonging to one of the police outriders was lying across the road. The glare of a hi-vis jacket lying under the car in front was stomach-churning but explained why their driver had swerved so suddenly, trying to avoid a further accident.

She got to her feet and saw Amir's parents being led over to the side of the road, seemingly uninjured but understandably shaken.

'Are you okay? What about Soraya and Raed?' There was no sign of the other cars or carriage, which had been in front.

'We're okay and I don't think the others even know what's happened, they were so far ahead of us. It's that poor policeman who's been hurt.' Djamila was visibly upset and Isolde guessed that she'd witnessed the accident.

'Amir and Farah are in the back of the car if you want to see them. They're fine but we're trying to keep her calm. I think it's brought back a lot of difficult memories for her. I'll go and see what I can do to help here.' Isolde left them and rushed over to where a small crowd had gathered on the ground around the injured outrider.

'Can I help?' she asked, kneeling down on the road, every speck of gravel digging into the skin on her knees through what was left of her flimsy dress. Not that it mattered. The pain was simply a reminder that she was alive. The shock and whatever other after-effects of the crash were still to manifest would likely show up later once the adren-aline had worn off. For now, however, she was simply glad that all of her loved ones were safe.

'Sweetheart, you'll be safe with your grand-parents. I know this is scary but we're all okay. I need to go and help the man that was injured.' Amir didn't want to leave Farah, he knew this was bringing back so many bad memories, but he also knew there was some-one out there who needed him more right now. His mother and father had recounted the accident to him and the fact that Isolde was out there dealing with everything on her own.

'In case he has a little girl who needs him too?' Farah asked, her big wide eyes tugging violently on his heartstrings. It was apparent that she was worried some other innocent child was about to lose a parent and have her world turned upside down. Not if he could help it.

'Exactly,' he said, swallowing down all that love he had for his daughter for now so he could provide some assistance. Later, once he knew he'd done everything he could, he might just hug her and never let go.

Farah nodded and went to his mother, freeing him to leave the relative comfort and safety of the car. He found Isolde halfway under the car in front tending to the accident victim.

'What can I do to help?' He ducked his head under the chassis of the car to offer his assistance.

Isolde turned slightly to see him, her face smeared with dirt and grease. 'This is Mike. The front wheels of the car have gone over him. He's conscious, pulse is a little fast, breathing is a little shallow, and he's experiencing serious pain in his chest. He can't move his hand. It looks as though his fingers have been crushed.'

'The paramedics will be able to give you something for that pain when they get here. In the meantime, let's try and make you more comfortable.' Easier said than done given the circumstances as it was difficult to get access to the patient and assess his condition. Crush injuries had a high risk of death if not treated immediately, and, though they were at the mercy of the paramedic's response time, Amir would do what he could.

He called over all the drivers and members of security that had been travelling with the family. 'We need to try and lift the car off Mike. Isolde, before we do that can you make a tourniquet around his wrist?'

With a quick flick of his wrists he undid his tie and passed it to Isolde for a makeshift tourniquet. If blood flow was restricted or impaired for more than fifteen minutes toxins could be released into the bloodstream and cause kidney failure.

'Okay, done.'

'Now I need you to hold his head steady as you can and we'll do our best to make it a clean lift.'

There was no room for mistakes here. They needed to lift the car straight up and over, away from Mike, and without jarring him at all. It was a precarious situation and they didn't know the extent of his injuries. One knock could cause paralysis, but with no idea how long it would take the emergency services to get here Amir thought they had to do something.

'We're ready,' she shouted back so he knew she was in place to watch their patient and make sure they didn't cause him any further injury in their attempt to help him.

'Okay. On the count of three I want everyone to lift. Then we'll shuffle over to the right until we're clear. Ready?' Amir was at the back of the vehicle with some of the others, more positioned around the side of the car, all hands under the chassis, ready to lift. It was said that in extreme circumstances adrenaline could propel a man to lift a car single-handed but he was hoping there were enough of them to manage it without relying on a myth.

'One, two, three…' Using every ounce of effort he possessed verbalised in a grunt, he took the strain along with the others.

'All good,' Isolde shouted up from underneath to let them know it had been a successful operation so far. With her at risk too if they lost their grip and dropped the car, Amir dug deep for his inner bodybuilder. He mightn't have the same bulky physique as the security guys, but he certainly had all the heart.

They shuffled in unison across the road

until they were clear of Mike and Isolde on the grass.

'On the count of three, drop and step away.' He didn't want anyone injured by a car falling on them because they were in a rush. They had to do this carefully and methodically.

'One, two, three…' He pulled his hands free and stepped back, watching to make sure everyone else had done the same. Once they were sure it had been a success whoops and hollers filtered into the air along with the back-slaps. Amir didn't wait for congratulations, moving quickly over to the pair left lying in the middle of the road.

'Are you both okay?' he asked, now he could see the couple more clearly. Isolde was stretched out lying on her belly tending to the injured policeman, her beautiful dress now ripped and covered in dirt.

'I'm okay, but Mike has lacerations and contusions all over.' Now the car had been lifted away Isolde was able to sit up and talk while staying close to the patient.

Amir knelt down to take a preliminary look but it wasn't easy to see the injuries clearly, given the position Mike was lying in and because he was still wearing his protective clothing. 'Mike, I know you're uncomfortable at the minute but we don't want to move you or take your helmet off in case we exacerbate any injuries. What we will do is try and stabilise you so the paramedics can transfer you quickly and safely to the hospital when they get here.'

He stood up again to address those standing around watching. 'Can we get some blankets, water, and if anyone has a first-aid kit to hand it would be helpful.'

The crowd of men dispersed and disappeared back into the convoy of cars to retrieve any useful items. In the meantime Amir took off his jacket and covered the policeman to try and keep him warm. There was a very real chance of his body going into shock and causing all manner of complications.

'Are you hanging in there, Mike?'

'Just tired...' he mumbled in response.

'Please try and stay awake. There's a real chance you could have suffered a concussion when you hit the ground and we need to keep you conscious for now. They'll be able to monitor you better at the hospital. It won't be long until the ambulance gets here.' Amir did his best to keep the man talking. Falling asleep now could mask any complications such as a brain injury. At least in the hospital they would be able to treat any complications.

Some of the drivers and security men returned with blankets and bottles of water. Amir covered Mike first to try and keep him warm, then handed another blanket and some water to Isolde.

'What do you want to do about that hand?' she asked, taking a swig from the bottle.

'We need to elevate it above the heart to reduce pain and swelling.' Amir was about to do just that when another driver handed him a small first-aid kit. He pulled out a disposable ice treatment pack and some bandages.

'Mike, I'm going to apply an ice pack to these fingers. It might be uncomfortable at first but it should numb the pain in that area.' He broke the ice pack to activate it and wrapped it in the bandages so it wouldn't cause any burns to Mike's skin and gently pressed it against his fingers, which were now beginning to swell and bruise.

The policeman drew a sharp intake of breath but let Amir proceed. He knew there were likely more serious injuries going on, but it was going to take careful handling and X-rays at the hospital to determine the extent of the damage.

'Mike? Stay with us.' Isolde suddenly sounded very concerned and began gently patting the policeman's face, which had turned grey, and he wasn't responding.

Amir checked Mike's pulse and, when he couldn't find it, tore open his clothing to listen to his chest. Nothing. 'He's gone into cardiac arrest. We're going to have to perform CPR.'

As he was a surgeon most of his work was undertaken in the operating theatre, where it was controlled and chock-full of medical equipment for unforeseen situations like this. Unfortunately, there were no defibrillators available out here in the middle of nowhere, so until the ambulance came it was all down to him and Isolde.

'What do you need me to do?' Though emergency medical intervention wasn't her expertise either, he knew she'd see it through with him.

'I'll start chest compressions. On the count of thirty, you do the rescue breaths. Hopefully help will arrive soon.' Without further delay, Amir put the heel of his hand in the middle of Mike's chest, interlocked the fingers of his other hand, and with arms locked began to push down.

'One, two…' He counted with every compression until he reached thirty and paused.

At which point Isolde tilted Mike's head up, pinched his nose, and placed her lips around his open mouth. She blew until his chest rose, then repeated the action. Then it was Amir's turn again. They continued, not knowing if there was any internal bleeding, but determined to get his heart beating again.

His arms were beginning to tire and he was on the brink of asking Isolde to swap over when he saw Mike's chest rise by itself.

'Stop!' he shouted before Isolde gave another rescue breath and leaned down to listen to the man's chest.

'He's breathing.' The sheer relief had him welling up that their efforts hadn't been in vain as he rolled Mike into the recovery position.

'Thank goodness.' Isolde threw her arms around him and hugged him.

He knew it was because she was as relieved as he. It was an act of solidarity and a release from the pressure of having this man's life in their hands. He enjoyed it all the same. Not just the warmth of her in his arms, but having a partner again, someone to share his life experiences with. With an extra helping of guilt, he also realised the reason he enjoyed being with Isolde so much was because she accepted him, appreciated him, co-operated with him. All the things his wife hadn't always been keen to do. When he was around Isolde he felt loved, and it was an intoxicating dilemma always wanting to be around her, yet knowing nothing could come of it.

She was the one to let go first, backing away slowly with a look of regret in her eyes.

'The ambulance is going to be here very soon, Mike,' she soothed their patient, and Amir knew she would wait with him until the last second when they transferred his care over to the paramedics.

He was sure it came as a relief all round when the sirens were heard approaching.

Once Amir had passed on all the details of Mike's condition to the ambulance crew, he focused his attention on Isolde, who was looking a little bit worse for wear. As he was sure he did too.

'You should go and get checked at the hospital too. I know you hurt yourself getting out of the car.' He could see the tears in her dress and the cuts on the exposed skin where she'd struggled to get out of the car in her determination to go and help.

Isolde most definitely was not a pernickety princess afraid of getting her hands, or clothes, dirty. She was courageous, selfless and unbelievably kind. He didn't know why she thought she wouldn't be suited to motherhood when it was clear she was a natural nurturer. The responsibility she claimed she didn't want was there in every action she took to look after others.

Still, it wasn't any of his business when it was clear there couldn't be anything between them, and therefore not an issue. They just had to make sure Farah understood that too. Her earlier comments were concerning and he didn't want her to get ideas in her head that Isolde was going to become part of their little family. If anything, once they were back in England they'd probably have to put more distance between them, at least in their personal lives. He didn't want Farah to be disappointed so he'd probably have to have a word with her later and put her straight on the nature of their relationship. Something they'd had trouble deciphering but now realised had no future as anything other than colleagues.

They'd initially moved to England as a

family after Farah was born. He'd had a soft spot for the country since he'd studied there and he wanted her to have the best education. She'd been enrolled in a top private school before she could even talk. In hindsight he'd probably thought it would be a new start for all of them, the cracks already beginning to show in the marriage, but he guessed it, like him, hadn't lived up to his wife's expectations.

She'd wanted glitz and glamour, and to be social climbers. He hadn't. She'd thrown it back at him that night before driving off, telling him he was boring and unambitious. Laughable, when he'd been lined up to take over the throne in Zaki. England had simply been his last chance for a quiet family life before he took up his real duties. So he'd shied away from the society life, following Raed's example. In a way he envied his older brother's anonymous, normal life, though going home had never been in question for Amir. He always did the right thing. Even when it wasn't always what he wanted.

Like now. What he really wanted was to be back with his family with support and company, but he knew Farah was getting the best treatment with Isolde in London. She'd already come so far, he didn't want to set her back by upsetting her routine. However, he would have to be careful she didn't read more into Isolde's presence in their lives than her being Farah's physiotherapist.

'It's just a few cuts. Nothing to worry the health service over. A shower and a change of clothes and I'll be as right as rain. It's just as well Farah and I had designed equally fabulous outfits for the reception.' She looked forlornly at her ruined dress, which he knew had taken a lot of work on her behalf. It said a lot about her that she'd been willing to sacrifice it to help someone else.

'Speaking of whom…' His mother and father were walking towards them pushing Farah in her wheelchair, now that she'd been given the all clear by the emergency services.

'Papa!' Farah threw her arms around his waist and hugged him tight.

'Hey. Everyone is safe,' he said, stroking her hair, grateful that she'd been spared in the accident that had taken her mother, but sorry she'd had to experience the trauma again.

'What…about…the…policeman?' she hiccupped through sobs.

Amir's heart lurched. It was a sign of how much her mother's death had affected her that she was so worried about a stranger's family having to go through the same thing.

'He's going to be all right, Farah. The ambulance is going to take him to hospital and they'll make sure he's okay.' Isolde crouched down at eye level with Farah and did her best to reassure her too. Only to have Farah launch herself at her next, almost knocking her over in the process. He saw Isolde wince when she wrapped her arms around her and squeezed.

'Careful,' Amir warned but Isolde waved away his concern.

'She's fine. I'm fine. We're all fine. So I suggest we make our way to the party before my sister loses her mind completely.' It was only now she'd thought to check her phone, kindly retrieved from the car with her bag by Djamila. The numerous texts, missed calls and voice messages would suggest Soraya had heard about the accident.

'I did tell her none of us were hurt,' Djamila interjected. No doubt she'd had a billion calls too, but Isolde knew nothing would pacify her sister other than seeing for herself. Thankfully they weren't too far from the palace or she was likely to turn that carriage around and race back.

'That's big sis, overprotective and made

to worry. I'll just send a quick text to confirm I'm still alive.' Isolde knew Soraya was going to make a great mother some day because she was so good at it already. She'd benefitted from her sister's love and support her entire life, and now it was time to let her have her own life instead of worrying about her all the time.

Tonight had given her a taste of what it was like to feel that kind of fear only a parent could go through when it seemed their child was in danger. Soraya might have been panicking that her little sister might have been injured, but Isolde's first thought had been for Farah's safety, and it hadn't just been in a professional capacity. The line had definitely been blurred between physiotherapist, friend, and something more that involved more emotions than she was prepared to deal with.

Given that the little girl was clinging to her too it was clear it wasn't a one-sided problem. Farah was too attached, figuratively and literally, and she was going to get hurt if Isolde remained in her life giving her false hope that she was somehow going to become a substitute mother figure. That was never going to happen. Better she made the break sooner rather than later instead of stoking the little girl's fantasy.

With one hand still holding onto Farah, Isolde deftly typed a quick message to Soraya with the other to assure her they were all safe and on their way to the palace.

Tonight she would hug her sister, get changed, and celebrate her nuptials. Because tomorrow she'd be gone.

CHAPTER SEVEN

AMIR CHECKED HIS phone for messages and took a note of the time. Farah and Isolde had been an age getting ready and he hoped it wasn't because she didn't want to come down again, or she had some sort of delayed shock after the accident. Farah hadn't wanted anyone but Isolde to help her get changed so he'd showered, put on a suit that didn't look as if it had been in a car wreck, and come down to the reception party. Now he was sitting foot tapping at the table waiting for their big entrance and a sign that his daughter hadn't been retraumatised by today's events.

Soraya and Raed had rushed to meet them the second they'd reached the palace, barely letting them get out of the car before swarming around them to make sure they hadn't downplayed the incident. Once he and Isolde had assured them all they needed was to shower and change they'd finally agreed to go ahead with the reception. Though they'd already apparently told their assembled guests what had happened, extolling their bravery and heroics, they'd insisted on putting the evening on hold until the whole family were together. His mother and father had since made their appearance but they were all listening to the DJ's filler music until the real party started.

He stopped Soraya as she moved between guests, his anxiety getting the better of him. 'Should I go up and see what's keeping them?'

'Listen, if there's one thing my sister hates, it's being rushed. Relax, Amir, they'll be here soon. She would have told you if there had been any problems with Farah. Don't worry. They're just making sure they look good for you.'

The knowing wink she gave him before moving on to mingle with the rest of the guests did nothing to alleviate his restlessness. Things were already difficult without the whole family thinking there was something going on between him and Isolde. Simply wishing it into existence didn't make it work. If anyone knew that, it was him. From the outside it probably seemed so easy for them to be together when they spent so much time in each other's company already, and Farah trusted her, liked her, and more importantly was comfortable around her. It was him who'd messed things up, and now he had to take all of that away from her to protect both of them from more pain long term.

As he fidgeted with the edge of the linen tablecloth he had a sudden urge to look up. The whole room seemed to fall silent and his hands stilled as Isolde and Farah entered the room. His daughter was wearing a pretty baby-blue jumpsuit. She'd been careful to keep her legs covered but the light crepe material, ruffled at the top with puffed sleeves, and embellished with embroidered sparkly butterflies, still made her look like the princess she was. Despite her carefully co-ordinated ivory bag and shoes, crepe bow in her hair, the prettiest accessory she wore was her smile. And of course the fairy wings Isolde had encouraged her to wear.

'I hope we didn't keep everyone waiting too long,' Isolde whispered as she wheeled Farah over to the table.

'It was worth the wait,' Amir said diplomatically, meaning every word. He would have sat here all night just to be rewarded with the utter happiness radiating from his daughter, her earlier distress hopefully now a distant memory.

He kissed Farah on the cheek and it felt only natural to do the same with Isolde. Although the second he made contact that electricity sparked straight back to life, singeing his lips where he'd touched her skin.

'Do I look all right? This wasn't how I started the day...' Isolde glanced around the room, patting her hair into place and tugging at the hem of her dress.

'You look beautiful.' He didn't have to lie to make her feel better when she was as stunning as ever. The hair, which had been scraped back into an elegant updo earlier, was now hanging loose around her shoulders, a little damp at the ends from her rush to join the party. She was back to her minimal make-up, which he personally preferred to the full mask she'd sported for the official photographs, looking more like herself. As for the cobalt-blue dress...it was stunning.

'We fairies try our best.' She twirled around so he could see the wings she was wearing to match Farah's. It didn't matter to her what anyone thought except Farah and he adored her for that.

Amir took a step back as the words his subconscious conjured hit him in the gut as well as the heart. He was glad when the music started and the bride and groom were called to the floor for their first dance as husband and wife, because he didn't think he was capable of speech in that moment. Despite all the soul-searching and promises not to kiss Isolde again, he'd fallen for her anyway, and he didn't know what to do about it.

As he watched the loved-up newly-weds sway together on the floor he envied their uncomplicated relationship. He wished things were as easy for him and Isolde to be together without the spectre of impending doom haunting their every move.

Raed left his dance partner briefly to speak to the DJ and grinned at Amir. It was only when the DJ called for the chief bridesmaid and best man to come to the floor that he realised why. He wasn't going to let his baby brother fade into the background despite his best efforts. There was a round of applause, someone pushed him forward, and Farah urging, 'Dance with Isolde, Papa,' leaving him with no choice.

'May I?' he asked, holding out a hand for Isolde.

'You may.' She took his hand and let him lead her onto the dance floor, leaving Farah with her grandparents watching from the sidelines.

The slow number left them nowhere to hide, their bodies pressed tightly together as they let the music carry them across the dance floor.

'Good to see you enjoying yourself, brother.' Raed nudged him with his elbow as they passed each other.

Amir gave a strained smile. This was not fun, it was torture. Her breath at his ear, her breasts pushed against his chest and the strands of her hair brushing against his cheek were driving him crazy.

'Sorry,' Isolde whispered into his ear, making the hairs on the back of his neck to attention. He felt bad for making it obvious he was uncomfortable.

'You've nothing to be sorry for.' To try and prove the point he pulled her even closer. It wasn't her fault he couldn't get a handle on his emotions when he was in her orbit. Especially when she'd given him a million reasons to be grateful.

'Thank you for everything you've done for Farah today. The outfits were amazing.

You're a woman of many talents. I can't remember the last time my daughter looked so happy.' She was sitting singing along to the music with his parents, looking like any other child enjoying the party. Miles away from the frightened young girl who'd first met Isolde, struggling to deal with her life-changing injuries and not even wanting to be seen in public. She'd surprised everyone today with her bravery.

'I can't take all the credit. I think a lot of the changes in her are down to her devoted father too. It just takes time to process everything she's been through. I see it a lot in my line of work.'

He did too but perhaps because this was so close he hadn't seen the changes in her until now. It was a slow transition but gradually she was getting back to the little girl she used to be. He knew Isolde was a lot to do with that even if she was reluctant to accept a starring role.

It also hadn't been lost on him that her first concern when the crash happened had been for Farah, and she'd come to comfort her once they'd dealt with the patient. He knew why she was reluctant to get close, given her background, he knew why he was afraid of letting her get too embedded into their lives, but he couldn't seem to accept it. Fate seemed to be pushing them together at every turn and his resistance was getting lower by the second. He just wished they didn't have to keep this safety barrier erected between them and could simply enjoy being together.

The slow song ended to a round of applause, followed by a faster pop number, which meant he had to reluctantly loosen his hold on Isolde before it became too obvious he didn't want to let go.

'I think there's someone else who wants to dance with you.' Isolde went to get Farah and wheeled her onto the dance floor as everyone else made their way up to join in.

Amir walked over to meet them, but Isolde quickly dodged around in front of Farah's wheelchair and placed a hand on his chest to stop him. 'Just wait here. Farah has something planned for you both.'

He had no idea what they were up to but they'd clearly been working on something other than dresses behind the closed doors and conspiratorial giggles. Nevertheless, he did as he was told and waited patiently to see what they had in store for him next.

He watched as Isolde kicked away the foot

stand on Farah's wheelchair, then proceeded to lift her out. His first instinct was to rush over and grab her before she fell over. They'd been here before, every time a knock to her confidence and setting her recovery back even further. However, he trusted Isolde. She wouldn't do anything to humiliate him or his daughter in public like this, and she'd said it was Farah's idea. If his daughter had plucked up the courage to do something in front of everyone it was a major progression and he wasn't going to stop her. All he could do was be there for her if she needed him.

His heart was in his mouth as Isolde manoeuvred Farah onto her feet and slowly let go until she was standing on her own two feet. Her legs were shaking with the effort but her smile made him want to weep with pride. Then she started to walk and he couldn't hold back the tears. This was everything he and Isolde had been working for and his amazing, brave daughter had chosen tonight to prove the effort had all been worth it.

With Isolde right by her side Farah took a couple of shuffling steps forward, her eyes completely focused on him. It reminded him of when she'd taken her very first steps at just over a year old. She had that same determination to reach him, her body trying to keep up with her will. When she stumbled both he and Isolde rushed to catch her, but her smile was just as bright.

'I did it, Papa,' she said, pride and hope shining in every word that this was only the start and some day she wouldn't need the wheelchair at all.

'Yes, you did, my brave, brilliant girl.' He kissed the top of her head, tears soaking his face.

Amir could hear the gasps of astonishment all around as the guests and wedding party witnessed the miracle along with him. Farah looked tired but he knew his daughter, she wouldn't want to end the moment too early.

'She's been working on this for a while. She wanted to surprise you,' Isolde said with a hint of wariness in her voice. No doubt she'd struggled over not telling him about Farah's progress, but it was more important to him that she'd kept Farah's confidence and provided her with a friend who could be trusted.

'You certainly did that, but I don't want you to overexert yourself too quickly. Isolde, could you help position Farah so she's standing on my feet?' That way he could take the strain and do his best to hold her up without losing the moment.

Isolde went one better. Not only did she get Farah closer to him, she stood behind her, keeping her upright and resting her hands on her hips, so the three of them were ostensibly dancing together. It didn't matter it wasn't in time to the music or particularly energetic, Amir was dancing with his daughter. Something he'd thought he'd never get to do ever again. And suddenly their whole future looked so much brighter with possibilities. He pulled her close, then went in for a full group hug to include Isolde, the three of them doing little more than swaying to the music together but it was perfect.

When the song was over he carried Farah back to her wheelchair, telling her they had to take one step at a time. As soon as she was settled the rest of the family came to hug her and tell her how proud they were of her, tears abounding.

'I should take her up to bed, she's exhausted,' he told everyone when he noticed her yawn.

'Your father and I can settle her and then rejoin the party. We have the room.' His mother's offer was a welcome reminder that as long as they were here he didn't have to do everything on his own. He had support.

'I'm sure she would much rather sleep in her own bed. You want me to come up with you, Farah?'

She shook her head. 'You stay here.'

Her glance flicked between him and Isolde and he could see she hadn't given up on her idea of getting them together. At this moment he didn't want to do anything to burst her bubble.

'You stay and enjoy yourselves,' his mother insisted, collecting his father and Farah before making a gracious exit.

'On a scale of one to ten, how mad at me are you?' Isolde asked as they watched the others leave.

'Zero,' he said honestly. 'Of course I would've wanted to know she was back on her feet, but I wouldn't wish away the smile it put on her face when she surprised me.'

'She's worked hard.'

'As have you. Between making the dresses and helping her to walk again, you've had your work cut out for you.'

'I'm happy if she's happy. That's all I can ask for.' Isolde's words were said by good parents the world over, always wanting the best for their children. Although he could never say that. It would send her running if she thought for one moment anyone saw her as a mother figure. Amir saw her as much more but he knew it was the one role that would scare her away.

'Well, we both thank you.'

He heard her take in a small breath, as though she was about to say something, then without warning she reached up and hugged him. It had been an emotional moment for both of them, but there was something so final in that embrace he didn't want to let go.

'Why don't we both go and get a drink?' Whatever she'd been about to say he knew he wasn't ready to hear it, wanting the euphoria of the evening to continue as long as possible.

Instead of trying to catch the attention of the busy waiters, he made his way to the bar with Isolde in tow.

'You kept that quiet.'

'Such a brave little girl.'

'You should be very proud.'

As they waited for their drinks it seemed everyone who'd witnessed the father-daughter dance wanted to offer their support and congratulations. Although it was very kind, it was also overwhelming. He needed some space to process everything too.

Grabbing the two glasses of champagne that eventually appeared on the bar top and gesturing for Isolde to follow him, he made his way to the French doors at the back of the room. She opened the doors so he didn't spill their drinks in an awkward attempt to do it himself and they stepped out onto the patio away from the crowd.

'I needed some air,' he explained, perching on the top of the steps that led down to the vast manicured gardens.

Isolde sat down beside him and accepted the champagne offered to her. 'Understandable. Today has been a lot.'

'Here's to surviving,' he said, raising his drink in a toast.

Isolde clinked her glass to his. 'I'm sorry for not telling you about Farah, and for…you know, hugging you.'

'Will you stop apologising? It was a big moment. I lost serious man points back there by blubbing over my baby.'

'We were all in tears, Amir. It would've looked kinda weird if you hadn't been moved. I think Farah did it on purpose to make a show of you in public.'

He knew she was joking but so was he. When Farah had taken those first wobbly steps towards him he hadn't cared about anyone else in the room, except perhaps for Isolde who was very much part of it all.

'I didn't think Soraya and Raed had eyes for anyone other than each other. I'm surprised they noticed.'

Isolde slapped him playfully on the arm. 'Don't be mean. They're happy.'

'Yeah, it's sickening, isn't it?' He tossed back the champagne, swallowing the bubbles before they had time to go up his nose.

'No, it's lovely.' She laughed, refusing to get drawn into his pity party.

'I know. I'm just jealous that they get to be together and we can't.' Perhaps it was the events of the day that had worn down his defences, the glass of champagne helping him to say what he was feeling without overthinking the consequences.

'We're here now.' Isolde bumped affectionately against him but it only made Amir want more than a glancing touch between them.

He set his glass on the step, took Isolde's and did the same with hers, before taking her hands in his. 'You know what I mean, Isolde. We like each other, I don't think that's in doubt, and apparently our mouths are magnetised or something since they always seem to be drawn together.'

'Amir…we've been through this. There's Farah to think about, and us. We both know how this ends.' She rested her forehead against his.

'Why do we have to think about anything? Why can't we just enjoy ourselves like everyone else here? For weeks we've been doing the right thing and setting aside what we want. When do we get to have some fun? Why can't we just have a drink and a dance without the weight of everyone else's expectations dragging us down?'

Amir got to his feet and pulled Isolde up with him. He'd had his fill of trying to be perfect and tempering his actions to be mindful of other people's feelings. Just for once he wanted to be himself, to do what he wanted, and feel without limits.

He began to dance, twirling Isolde around before pulling her back into hold, one hand resting on her back, the other clasping her hand between their bodies. She gasped and laughed at the impulsive move, only making him want to do it more. He dipped her back, her eyes staring up at him with such vulnerability and trust that made her parted lips too irresistible.

The kiss happened because he wanted it to and because he knew she wanted it too. The soft touch of her mouth against his was his reward for braving a step out of his comfort zone but it was over too quickly when Isolde broke it off and pushed up on his chest. He'd got it wrong again.

'I'm sorry—'

'Let's not go through this again. When it comes to kissing you I am a very willing participant,' she said with a smile that managed to soothe his guilty conscience before it overwhelmed him again.

'But it can't happen again. I get it.'

Isolde faced him with her hands on her hips. 'Will you please stop answering for me? What I was going to say was if we're going to…indulge ourselves, I'd rather not do it in public. If this is going to be a one-off we don't need witnesses who'll read too much into it. Right?'

'Right.' Amir was reeling from her reaction, trying to understand what was happening.

She took him by the hand, leading him back inside.

'Where are we going?'

Isolde didn't answer him until they'd ducked through to the other side of the busy room and out into the hallway. 'I think the best man and bridesmaid are expected to get it on at a wedding, then never speak about it again.'

'You mean…one night together?' He didn't dare believe that was what she was suggesting in case he'd read everything wrong again.

'If that's what you want?' Isolde's earlier display of confidence wavered as she bit her lip waiting for him to respond.

'I want,' he said, unable to stop himself reaching for her, holding her face in his hands so he could kiss her without restraint.

If one night was all they were going to get, he would take it. It was better to show her how he felt for a limited time than to never get the chance. No one had to know, would force their expectations for what happened next between them, or had to suffer the consequences of things not working out. It would be their secret. Their time together. Though he wanted longer, more than one night, just maybe it could be enough to persuade her they had a future together.

* * *

Now all bets were off Isolde knew they were in danger of getting carried away. It was as though they'd finally unleashed everything they'd been feeling for one another, everything they'd been trying to keep under wraps, in that one kiss.

'I think we should go to my room before there are rumours of another royal wedding happening.' She was only partly joking. As much as she was enjoying finally getting to have Amir without the guilt of her actions making things difficult, she could do without Soraya, or anyone else, seeing them making out and getting the wrong idea. She doubted the explanation that they were embarking on a one-night stand together because she couldn't commit would do either of their reputations any good.

'You're right. We shouldn't take any unnecessary risks.' Amir grabbed hold of her hand and practically sprinted to the top of the stairs in his haste to get to her room. In the end she had to kick off her heels to catch up with him, running barefoot, her shoes dangling from her fingers as they ran through the palace corridors like two horny teenagers.

When he'd confessed to wanting a brief

respite from all of his worry and responsibility to his family, Isolde had been able to relate. It was nice to have the opportunity to be reckless and impulsive again even for a short while, not having to be on her guard. The chemistry between her and Amir had always been there, occasionally boiling over into a passionate encounter. Until now they'd been fearful about acting upon it, guilty when they had. She was looking forward to that freedom to display her emotion and do what she wanted with Amir. The very thought sent shivers of delight along her spine.

He'd surprised her with the idea that they should get a little reckless, and she'd taken that idea and run with it, until they were heading towards a night together. Heaven. She'd had a little wobble of confidence when she thought about what this represented to Amir. Although she wasn't privy to all the details of his personal life, she was pretty sure this was the first time he'd been with anyone since his wife had died. That was a huge step for him and something they hadn't talked about in this sudden rush to be together. It was a milestone for him, one that he might not have even considered yet. What she didn't want was for him to assign any more significance to this than a one-night stand, because the idea of this was to avoid any hurt, not make things worse.

Before she opened her bedroom door she paused to make sure this was genuinely what he wanted, that he wasn't going to confuse this for something other than a physical release. They couldn't afford to get involved in anything emotional, which was why turning this into a meaningless fling was the only way to make it work.

'Amir, I really want this, I do, but are you sure? I mean, are you ready to move on, albeit temporarily?' She traced her fingers over the exposed skin at his throat where he'd opened his top button and loosened his shirt, trying to keep things flirty, despite the seriousness of the question.

Amir stopped her wandering fingers with one hand, his brown eyes holding her captive. 'I'm sure.'

He didn't get into the details of why he was so sure, and if she was honest it did niggle a bit that he wasn't going to explain so they both knew why he was so certain. However, as he backed her against the door and kissed her hard, letting his hands skim along her body, all her worries fled. She was already turned on but as he stroked the bare skin of her thighs she went into meltdown.

It had been a while for her too. Perhaps that was why she wanted to make sure they didn't assign more significance than a hook-up. If she thought about it too much she might realise it was a bad idea because Amir was the furthest thing from being a meaningless hook-up. Her sister had just married into his family, they were colleagues, she was treating his daughter…there were so many emotional connections. And that didn't even include the feelings she knew she already had for him. Then he slid his hand under her dress, into her panties, and she didn't care any more.

They stumbled into her room and she dropped her shoes onto the floor to leave her hands free to undress him. Amidst a frenzy of kisses and trembling fingers she eventually managed to strip him of his shirt so she could slide her hands over the hard planes of his torso, mapping every muscle to memory. Amir unzipped her dress, the sensation of his fingers tracing the line of her spine making her skin tingle with arousal. Her dress fell to the ground leaving her standing there in just her underwear. She should have felt vulnerable, exposed, but the hungry look in his eyes and his clearly physical reaction to seeing her half naked were enough to embolden her.

Isolde undid her bra and let it fall away. Her heart was racing with a mixture of anxiety and exhilaration about baring herself so completely to him, but he made her feel so sexy just with one look it wasn't long before her panties followed the rest of her clothes. She took a lot of satisfaction in seeing his Adam's apple bob as he swallowed hard watching her. Even more when he grabbed hold of her backside and pulled her close, crushing her against his hard body in his haste to kiss her again.

Isolde fumbled with the rest of his clothes, undoing his belt, opening his fly, and pushing away the last barrier between their naked bodies. The feel of his solid manhood pressed intimately against her made her breathless and slick with need.

Amir lifted her off the ground, hooking her legs around his hips, and backed her against the wall. She clung to him, her arms around his neck, her mouth clashing with his. It was the most intense, passionate display of mutual desire she could ever remember. The fact that they'd been holding back for so long was probably the reason it had exploded so spectacularly into this animalistic need for one another.

He palmed her breast and took her nipple into his mouth, sucking on the tip so hard she was teetering on the brink between pleasure and pain. She bucked against him with a gasp, not wanting him to stop as the sensitive nub grazed the roof of his mouth. Arousal swept over her until nothing else mattered except her need for him, her mind and body so attuned to what he was doing with his mouth that she ached for all of him.

It briefly crossed her mind that the reason it was so intense, so all-consuming, was because they had feelings for one another they were afraid to explore. This was always going to be more than a casual thing when there were emotions involved, real enough for her to try and run away from them. She knew that, but for tonight she didn't want to acknowledge it. There would be time for tears and self-recrimination another day. Now they were going to simply live in the moment.

'I need you,' she gasped at his ear, feeling him tighten against her in response.

'Now?' He searched her face, looking for

confirmation she was ready despite every part of her body telling him so.

'Now,' she said, wriggling against him until he was the one gasping with need.

Amir filled her with one thrust, taking their breath away, and making them smile at one another as though they'd just won the lottery. As her body adjusted to accommodate his thick erection she thought she had.

She buried her head against his neck, completely surrendering her body to him.

'You okay?' he asked, tilting her chin up so he could see her face.

'Yeah. More than okay,' she assured him, fighting the unexpected tears threatening to ruin the moment, reminding herself there were no emotions allowed. Apart from absolute euphoria, of course.

He kissed her again, this time a softer, more tender perusal of her lips, slowing the pace and giving them time to breathe again. It didn't make her want him any less and she ground her hips to his to deepen their connection further. Amir braced one hand on the wall, the other on the curve of her backside, as he drove into her, slowly filling her to satiate that need.

Sparks fired in her brain, all her nerve endings stimulated at once, overloading her body with sensation and making her quiver. He thrust again, grunting with effort into her ear. The sound was enough on its own to start that building pressure inside her searching for that final release.

She loved hearing those primal noises coming from a man so usually in control. It showed how much he wanted her, how much he needed this, and how passionate he was about her. As he carried her over to the bed she couldn't help but wonder how it would feel to have this every night to come home to. Knowing that this feeling of completeness was something Soraya and Raed had to look forward to for the rest of their lives, and she and Amir didn't.

It wasn't fair, but life never had been for either of them. All they could do was grab this moment of happiness with both hands and have the memory to cherish long after they'd parted ways. The problem was everything Amir was doing to her, making her feel, could never be replicated. It was the first and last time she'd ever get to experience it. If it was punishment for her decision to remain child-free she was certainly going to make sure she enjoyed her freedom first.

* * *

If this was the only time they'd have together to explore those feelings they were both afraid to admit to, Amir wanted to make it last longer than a quick pounding against a wall. Regardless of his body insisting otherwise, a combination of his want for Isolde and because of how long it had been since he'd had this kind of release. She was everything he'd imagined and feared. Beautiful, sexy and energetic. The kind of partner in the bedroom every man wanted but only he was lucky enough to have. For tonight.

Something had changed between them then, the frantic urge to join together overtaken by something more meaningful. This was supposed to be a one-time thing, something to forget once they'd got it out of their systems. Yet as he looked at Isolde, feeling what he was feeling, this was no longer simply sex. He was making love to her. He wanted Isolde to know how he felt about her without actually saying the words and forcing her to run. As if continuing to pretend this was purely physical would protect them.

He knew all the reasons they shouldn't be together past tonight, but it didn't stop him from wishing for more. Now more than ever. If only Isolde could see herself the way he saw her, as a loving, caring woman who'd been burned in the past, she might be able to see a future for them. There was no telling if it would work out for them long term, but Amir was willing to try rather than lose her altogether.

Apparently sensing his mood change, Isolde kissed his neck, sliding her hand between their bodies to stroke the most intimate part of him so he couldn't think too deeply any more, that animal part of him coming back to the fore. Tomorrow he would try and talk to her. Tonight was about actions, not words.

He pulled away and flipped Isolde so she was on her hands and knees, facing away, presenting her sweet backside towards him. Amir gripped her hips and slid easily inside her wet channel. Her little satisfied groans and the sexy look she cast him over her shoulder stole the last of his control. As he thrust forward, she pushed back, and they rode that final peak together until the room echoed with their cries of ecstasy. He was thankful the other rooms were a considerable distance away, given that they were supposed to be keeping this rendezvous secret, not announcing it to the world. His head was spinning, his body trembling as his climax hit. He lay down beside a smiling Isolde and reached over to give her a glancing kiss on the lips.

'Are you okay?'

'Better than okay,' she replied through panting breath, stroking her hand across his chest.

Even now, his body thoroughly sated, that simple contact was able to thrill him. He didn't think he'd ever tire of touching her, of being touched by her. It was just a shame it would end all too soon.

'I need a drink.' On unsteady legs he padded towards the mini fridge they kept stocked up in the rooms for guests and grabbed a bottle of water, his throat parched, lips dry. The refreshing ice-cold liquid went some way to aid his recovery from his exertions.

He climbed back onto the bed and passed the bottle to Isolde. She let out a sharp gasp as she spilled some onto her chest when she took a drink. A wicked idea began to form in Amir's head that he couldn't resist. He took a swig of the water, enough to cool his mouth completely, before leaning down and sucking Isolde's nipple into his mouth.

'Amir!' she gasped with the shock, though she was clearly loving it.

He licked the puckered tip, making her writhe beneath him, something he was getting way too addicted to already. With devilish glee he tipped a little more of the water out over her other nipple and watched it tighten with her squeal. Amir lapped the water dripping over her breast, teased her taut flesh with the tip of his tongue until it and he were hard. He simply couldn't get enough of her. So he was going to make sure they made enough memories tonight to last a lifetime.

Isolde woke to the sound of the shower running, and an empty bed. If she'd thought she could move she would've joined Amir under the water for some more passionate acrobatics. However, her body was refusing to cooperate, thoroughly sated and pleasantly numb from all their previous exhaustive antics. Instead she snuggled under the covers against the pillows, which now smelled of his cologne, never wanting to leave.

'Morning.'

The sound of his voice forced her eyes

open and she was rewarded with the sight of him walking, naked and wet, towards her. He dropped the towel he'd been using to dry his hair and slid in next to her. Regardless of her weariness she wanted him all over again. If she were lying on her deathbed she knew she'd still reach for him. Amir had made her feel things last night she'd never experienced before, a deep emotional connection that terrified but also made for out-of-this-world sex. She didn't want to leave this bed because she knew once she did it was all over, that she'd never get to have any of this—would never get Amir—ever again.

'Morning.' The thought that this could be the first and last time she got to wake up next to him made her bottom lip quiver a little so she covered it up by kissing him. A move that only made the moment even more bittersweet when he stroked her hair and kissed her tenderly in return.

'I've been thinking…'

She could see the excitement in the tension of his body and the shine in his eyes that he was building up to something and it didn't take much to guess what that was. Mistaking one night for the beginning of a relationship was exactly what she'd feared and warned him about from the start. They were supposed to part on reasonably good terms because they'd known going into this it was a one-time thing. She didn't want arguments and recriminations to be the lasting memory she had of their time together.

'Amir, don't. I know what you're going to say but sleeping together doesn't change anything.' Not their circumstances, but deep down she knew it had changed everything for her. No one else would ever come close to how he'd made her feel last night, and she knew no one could ever replace him in her affections. Her love life, if she ever deigned to have one again, would never recover.

'Are you honestly telling me you wouldn't want to do this again?' He was grinning at her, probably because he knew the answer to that question by her reluctance to leave the bed or tell him to go.

She narrowed her eyes at him. 'You know I would, but that wasn't the deal.'

It was that safety guard that had finally given her the excuse to act on her feelings. She hoped she wouldn't come to regret it when their time together had been even more than she could possibly have imagined.

Amir shuffled up into a sitting position.

'Hear me out. Soraya and Raed might be going on honeymoon but we're not due back at work until the end of the week. Why don't we stay here?'

'As much as I really, really enjoyed last night, I don't think I could survive on a diet of pure sex if we locked ourselves in for the next few days. Plus, your family might start to think something was wrong…' She had an idea of where he was going with this, but she didn't know if it was a good idea and tried to deflect the subject with humour.

It didn't work.

'I'm serious, Isolde. Although we don't have to be. I'm proposing to extend our casual arrangement for the duration of our stay here.'

'I don't want Farah to get hurt.'

'No one will have to know if you don't want. We managed to sneak away last night without causing a scandal. I'm sure we can do it again. I'll just ask Mother if Farah can stay in their rooms for an extra couple of nights so I can have some time to myself. Let's face it, it doesn't happen very often.'

'And this indecent proposal, would it have the same boundaries as last night? No complications, or expectations?' It was tempting to take him up on the offer of having a little more time together, the best of both worlds if they could continue exploring this amazing sexual chemistry without having to worry about anything long term. But she worried it was too good to be true.

'Listen, Isolde, if I thought there was a chance we could all live happily together for ever I'd take it. But we both know life isn't like that. You've made your feelings clear. Neither me, nor Farah, are in your long-term future.'

Isolde flinched at the bluntness of his words, and hoped that wasn't how it had come across when she'd tried to explain her reasons for not wanting anything serious with him. It was the only way she thought she could protect them all when she knew she could never measure up to the woman they both deserved in their lives.

'It's nothing personal, Amir. I'm just not cut out for the domesticity of family life. Ask my sister, she's still looking after me. What kind of mother would I be when I can't take care of myself?'

He was frowning at her now, all signs of his mischievous smile gone. 'I wish you wouldn't put yourself down like that. Yes, Soraya took care of you growing up because you were orphans, and she was your big sister. I know you were hurt in the past and perhaps that's clouding your view, but I see you, Isolde. You're a caring, responsible adult, whether you like it or not. If you don't want children that's entirely your prerogative, but don't put yourself down like that. There's no need to justify your feelings to me by denigrating yourself.'

Feeling thoroughly chastised now, Isolde whispered, 'Sorry.'

Amir caught her under the chin and tilted her face up to him.

'You don't have to say sorry to me for anything. You helped my daughter to walk again, for goodness' sake.' His light laugh told of his relief as well as his gratitude and Soraya suspected as soon as Farah opened her eyes he'd be checking in on her after last night's milestone.

'That's work though. I'm not so good with the emotional stuff.' She shrugged.

'I don't agree with you on that, but I guess that brings us back to where we started. If this is the only way I can have you, no strings, I'll take it. Even if it's only for a few more days. What do you say? Shall we upgrade from a one-night stand to a fling?'

He turned around so quickly from telling her she was a better person than she believed herself, to validating that idea she was only good for a good time, that her head was spinning trying to figure out who she was to him.

'Is that what you want, Amir?'

'It's all you're able to give me, isn't it?'

'Yes…yes, it is,' she reminded them both in case there was any future confusion. It wasn't going to do either of them any good wishing for the impossible. Instead they had to settle for reality. Or at least a version of it that would hopefully hurt less in the long run, and let them pretend they were getting this thing between them out of their systems.

As she reached for Amir again, her body coming alive again, hungry for more of him, she knew they were just fooling themselves that this could ever be enough. They were simply prolonging the inevitable, but she was too weak, too invested in what they did have to just walk away. Like every addict she had to wean herself off her particular drug of choice slowly, because going cold turkey would be too much of a shock to the system after the good time she was quickly getting used to.

CHAPTER EIGHT

'WHAT WOULD YOU like to do today, Princess?' Amir asked Farah as he poured himself a glass of orange juice.

He'd left Isolde to shower and dress and come down to breakfast with the rest of the family partly to avoid suspicion by appearing separately but also because he was famished. Last night, and this morning, had used up a lot of calories.

Not that he was complaining and he had to stifle a broad smile every time he thought of Isolde lying up there naked in his arms. He wished they were the ones jetting off on an exotic holiday together looking forward to sun, sea and lots of sex, leaving the rest of the world behind, instead of the happy couple making moon eyes at each other over the breakfast cereal. Neither he nor Isolde were ready for a honeymoon, but that time spent together in isolation sounded like bliss. He was lucky she'd agreed on another couple of days with him at least. It was probably the closest they'd get and he intended to enjoy every moment they had in private, but he wasn't going to neglect his daughter in the process.

'We're spending it together?' Her happy little face made the bite of toast he'd just taken feel like lead in his stomach. Even without last night's development with Isolde he'd spent more time away from her these past few days dealing with Fahid than he had in an entire year.

'Yes. It's your day, you get to choose what we do. I think you deserve it after all your hard work, even though it was naughty to keep secrets from your father.' He gave her a fake scowl, which didn't fool her in the slightest, probably because he'd sobbed like a baby over how proud of her he was last night.

'I wanted to surprise you, and I did,' she said casually, spooning her cereal into her mouth.

'You surprised us all, Farah,' Soraya added, making her grin at the notion it was more than her father she'd left flabbergasted.

'We're all very proud of you,' his father announced from the top of the table. He wasn't a man who often showed any affection, or praised anyone, so the comment did leave them all stunned for a moment.

Amir wondered if his near-death experience in England after his heart attack had made him appreciate his family more. Especially when they'd all worked so hard to keep things running during his illness and recuperation. If he'd ever told Amir he was proud of him, had made him feel good enough for the family he'd been born into, he might not have spent his whole life trying to prove himself worthy, or married someone he thought would impress them rather than someone he loved. It was too late to make amends with Farah's mother, but he hoped to end the toxic parent-child relationship that seemed to have plagued the royal family for years.

'So, what do you want to do? Manicures and mocktails, or rides at the amusement park?' That one might be a bit more difficult to pull off last minute, getting security in place for somewhere so public, but he reckoned he owed Farah some time, and a reward for all of her hard work. It would give her the incentive to keep going and hopefully progress even more. Although it was early days and he didn't want to put any pressure on her, he knew they were all hoping that some day she'd have full mobility back. That in the future they'd be able to look back on this time as a nightmare they survived.

The only good thing to come out of it all was meeting Isolde, and he knew even that time with her was limited.

'Morning.' She breezed into the dining room, washed, dressed, and not a hair out of place. As beautiful as she looked, he couldn't help think he preferred her naked with her hair in disarray, the way he'd left her in bed.

'Morning…' A chorus went up from around the table but he hoped the smile in response was solely for his benefit.

'I'm afraid we're nearly finished our break-fast and I have to go and finish packing, but we'll come and see you before we leave,' Soraya said, setting down her cup and get-ting up from the table just as Isolde sat down.

'Sorry, I slept in.' Isolde yawned.

'I didn't think you stayed that late last night. You'd disappeared before everyone left.'

Amir wondered if his absence had been noted too, or if it was considered anything other than a coincidence, but Soraya didn't as much as glance in his direction. The same couldn't be said for Isolde, who was watching him as she dug her spoon into her grapefruit, the juice spraying everywhere.

'I think it was all the excitement that kept me awake half the night.'

Amir almost choked on his toast and had to wash it down with more orange juice. So much for keeping things secret. He could feel his face flush with heat, imagining them all staring at him knowing full well why Isolde was exhausted. Though when he did look up the only person watching him was Isolde with that coy smile on her face that made him want to take her straight back up to bed again.

'The wedding, or our amazing girl?' Soraya asked, resting her hands on Farah's shoulders.

'Both. It's not easy keeping secrets, you know.' Isolde was playing with fire and someone was going to get burned if she wasn't careful. It was her idea to keep things quiet but it wouldn't take much for the others to catch on that she was talking about him, not Farah.

'We're going to do something special to celebrate today, aren't we, Farah?' He turned the conversation back to safer territory, and prayed Isolde would take the hint to stop teasing him.

'Oh, have you planned something nice?' Thankfully she turned her attention to Farah so he could breathe again.

His daughter thought for a moment before answering. 'I'd like to go to the beach.'

It was a simple request but one that surprised him. The beach was somewhere they'd liked to go as a family but since the crash he hadn't been able to persuade her to go. She'd been quite the water baby until the accident and hopefully this was a further turning point in her confidence.

'Anything you want, Princess.'

'I'm sure the kitchen will prepare you a hamper if you'd like,' his mother offered.

'Sounds great. Farah, why don't you go and write a list of all your favourites and we'll see if Chef can accommodate them for you?' Amir thought she deserved an extra-special treat for the courage with which she continually surprised him.

'Can Isolde come with us? To the beach, I mean?' His daughter's plea was so heartfelt that he didn't think he could decline her request without seeming petty. It wasn't that he didn't want to spend time with Isolde, or that he didn't want her intruding on his family time, but he wondered how he was going to manage to keep his burgeoning feelings for her under wraps.

It was one thing behind closed doors where they were free to explore those fresh emotions, but, as this breakfast had proved, hiding them around others was becoming increasingly difficult. Something they were going to have to resolve before they completely screwed the family dynamics. It would be difficult to treat this as a fling if everyone knew and expected more, and awkward once they returned to normal, meeting up at family gatherings with everyone party to their history. This would be a good test of their restraint.

'I'm sure your father would like to have you all to himself. I can stay here.' It was Isolde who provided the escape, declining the invitation so he didn't have to upset his daughter. Her empathy was one of the many things about her he appreciated. Though she often talked about being too selfish, he'd seen her put other people's feelings, especially Farah's, before her own.

'Nonsense. You haven't much time left, go and enjoy yourself. We won't be here as we have a prior engagement, and with Soraya and Raed heading off on their honeymoon it wouldn't be polite to leave you here on your own.'

'I'm sure I can find something to keep me occupied in a palace—' Isolde tried to appease his mother, who was concerned that their guest should be left alone, but Amir knew it was a wasted exercise.

'I won't hear another word. You've done so much for my granddaughter, and my son, it's the least we can do.' His mother rose from the table, matter settled as far as she was concerned. A continued rejection would be deemed an insult now and he was grateful Isolde seemed to realise that.

'In that case, thank you. I'd be delighted to go to the beach with you and your father, Farah.'

Amir saw the apology in Isolde's eyes when she looked at him and he acknowledged it with a smile, trying to reassure her it was okay. It wasn't her fault. Besides, getting to spend more time with Isolde was something to look forward to. It was the days when she wouldn't be there that he was dreading.

* * *

As the sea came into view through the car window Isolde didn't know who was more excited, Farah or her. It had been a long time since she'd had a beach holiday and working in London wasn't conducive to days at the seaside. She supposed it was the same for Amir and Farah, who'd been practically living at the hospital for the past year. They probably all needed a break and a chance to soak up some vitamin D. Although she hadn't originally been part of Amir's plan.

She didn't mind. After all, she'd monopolised him for most of the night and this morning, and he needed to spend time with his daughter. She suspected he'd also tried to make a clear distinction between his family life and their secret fling, which she appreciated since she didn't want the complication of anyone else finding out. Okay, so she'd had a little fun teasing him at breakfast, but only because she'd enjoyed seeing him get hot under the collar when she'd reminded him of their incredible night together. She knew she had to rein it in today around Farah. That didn't mean she hadn't chosen to wear an awesome bathing suit beneath her coverall that would totally rock his world.

'Looks like we're here. This is a spot the family owns so we shouldn't be disturbed.' As the car came to a standstill Amir unbuckled his belt and got out to retrieve Farah's wheelchair.

Isolde loved that he still did that even though they had people willing to do the heavy lifting for him. She knew it was because he was the kind of father who wanted to do everything he could for his daughter. The very reason they couldn't have more than a casual fling. Not only was she the wrong woman for his little family, but being with her would compromise the time he had with his daughter. She didn't want to do anything that could jeopardise the bond he had with Farah, especially when she wasn't going to be a long-term prospect for him.

Isolde helped unbuckle Farah and get her into the wheelchair. Although they'd made some progress she wasn't able to sustain her balance and mobility just yet and still needed some assistance. As frustrating as it was for Farah not to be back to her old self straight away, it was going to take more time and hard work. With her father's help, Isolde knew the little girl would get there. She couldn't help but wonder if she'd still be around to see it.

It wasn't a vast stretch of beach, but the little alcove had beautiful golden sand and a bank of surrounding trees making it private. Amir was able to ask security to keep a distance as no one could disturb them without being seen, and the party of three made their way onto the beach via a little wooden ramp she suspected had been added especially for Farah's use. The sunloungers and parasol awaited their arrival but Isolde couldn't wait to feel the sand beneath her toes and whipped off her sandals to paddle at the edge of the sea.

The cool water was refreshing and she scooped some up over her neck to try and lower her body temperature in the midday heat. When she turned back Amir was watching her intently, his jaw clenched, and she just knew he was thinking about last night. Now she was too, and counting the hours until she was back in his arms again. So much for cooling down.

'Would you like some pink lemonade, Isolde?' Farah had set out the contents of the picnic hamper they'd been given by the kitchen for their day out. She could get used to this level of pampering. Going back to her

one-bed flat alone was going to be so difficult for a multitude of reasons.

'Yes, thank you.' She came to join them at
the table positioned between the sunloungers
and helped herself to some of the salad and
cold meats spread out on platters.

Farah dutifully poured them all some of
the home-made pink lemonade, which they
drank greedily. Once she'd had her fill, Isolde
made herself comfy on her sunbed, with
Farah doing the same on hers. It was only
Amir who was sitting awkwardly on the edge
of his not looking relaxed in the least.

'Aren't you too warm, Amir? At least take
your shoes and jacket off.' Isolde stripped off
her loose floral coverall to reveal her red two-
piece bikini and felt Amir's eyes burning on
every exposed part of her skin.

'I'm fine,' he insisted gruffly.

Isolde took out the bottle of suncream
and applied it to Farah first so her shoulders
didn't get burned. Then she began rubbing it
into her own skin, smoothing it over her legs
and arms, before squirting it onto her chest.

'I'm going for a swim,' Amir announced,
hastily tugging off his T-shirt, kicking off his
trainers, and heading off barefoot towards the
edge of the sea.

Once he'd waded out waist-deep he dived in and swam away, his powerful strokes taking him further and further from the shore. Her little show, which she'd hoped would keep his interest stoked until they were able to be together in private later, had backfired. Now he was further away than ever.

'Will Papa be all right out there?' Farah asked anxiously and Isolde inwardly chastised herself again for crossing the line. There was something about Amir that made her walk that dangerous line even though they were supposed to be discreet. She couldn't seem to help herself when she was around him and that wasn't in keeping with the rules she had made in the first place.

'He looks like a very good swimmer but I'm sure he won't go far,' Isolde assured her, trying to convince herself too.

'I'd like to go in the water too,' Farah pronounced.

'Are you sure? Do you want to wait for your father to come back first?'

Farah shook her head displaying the same determination as her father. Isolde supposed the water would be good for her, taking the pressure off her limbs and giving her a sense of freedom.

'Okay. Put your arms around my neck and hold on tight.' Isolde decided it would be easier to carry her down to the water and she wasn't heavy.

With Farah in her arms she waded out, the cool water taking their breath away at first, but they soon acclimatised. In the distance Amir had turned around, perhaps seeing them in the water, and had begun swimming back. She was relieved, as was Farah apparently as she waved frantically, causing Isolde to nearly drop her in the process.

'I'm in the sea, Papa,' she shouted, though he was still too far away to hear.

Isolde manoeuvred her around, holding Farah under the arms and letting the water take the weight of her legs so she was essentially floating on the surface.

'You two look like you're having fun,' Amir said when he swam up to join them. His hair was slicked back with water, droplets beaded on his long dark eyelashes, and she'd had a nice view of his taut chest from the moment he'd peeled off his shirt. He was a beautiful man.

Farah beamed. 'I wanted to swim like you, Papa.'

Isolde saw the look of concern on Amir's

face that she was expecting too much. 'The buoyancy of the water is good for taking the pressure off her limbs. You could try and kick, Farah, if you want? It'll help strengthen your muscles.'

'I don't know if I can…'

'Try and come to me.' Amir reached out, encouraging Farah to close the small distance between them. It was all the encouragement she needed.

She launched herself at him, grabbing for his hands, splashing everyone in the process.

'Good girl. Now try kicking your legs out behind you.' Isolde moved to support her in case she couldn't manage to stay afloat. The last thing they wanted was for her to struggle and get swamped by the water, putting off any further attempts.

She could see the same determination on Farah's face as she had when they were working in secret to surprise her father. Whether Amir knew it or not his little girl idolised him and wanted to do it all to make him proud. When Isolde thought of her childhood and how little her parents were involved in it because of their illness, she realised exactly what she'd missed out on.

There were few memories of her father

except for coughing and sickness, hospital appointments and whispering behind closed doors. He hadn't been well enough to attend school plays or cheer her on during sports days. She had a vague recollection of her mum at a nativity play when she'd been an angel, but neither of them had been around during the high-school years. That had been Soraya.

Her parents hadn't been around and she didn't want the same for Farah. Today had proved she and Amir were incapable of separating their so-called 'no-strings fling' from his family life. They didn't need her screwing things up for them. She would be as guilty as her parents if she hung around knowing she wasn't capable of being the mother figure Farah needed, or the wife Amir deserved. Soraya might have been the best big sister anyone could have asked for, but they hadn't had the greatest role models. Isolde wouldn't know where to begin looking after a family, whereas Soraya had been doing it for most of her life. She wasn't about to do to Farah what her parents had done to them.

Farah had a devoted father and it wasn't fair of Isolde to take him away from her simply because she wanted him. That wasn't going to last for ever, as her last relationship proved all too well. Eventually Amir would see who she really was, once the rose-tinted glasses fell away, and leave her anyway. Everyone always did.

Staying here, lying to them both that no one would get hurt if they kept anything serious off the cards, was selfish and destructive. She'd had her fun and she didn't want to outstay her welcome. But this wasn't the time for that conversation. Not when Farah was on the brink of another revelation.

'That's it. Keep your head up, Farah, and kick those feet.' Amir bounced back another few feet to encourage her to go a little bit further, his heart about ready to burst with pride.

She'd come on so well these past months, fighting so hard to get her mobility back, and it was beginning to pay dividends. A year ago, when his life had seemed to be over, he could never have imagined her taking a few steps in front of a crowd, or trying to swim to him. Nor would he have believed he'd meet someone who accepted him for who he was without all his royal connections, or that he'd want to be with. Isolde was at the heart of the big changes that had happened in their lives for the better. He'd resisted the idea of a relationship because he didn't want to detract any attention from Farah, who'd needed him so badly, but Isolde was there for her just as much as he was.

Yes, she was clearly afraid of that level of commitment that came from being with someone who already had a child, but she was everything Farah needed too. The attraction between him and Isolde wasn't in question after last night, and the fact she'd agreed to continue their clandestine fling for a while longer told him she was interested in more than a normal one-night stand. He hoped, just maybe, by the end of this trip she would be as ready to take a risk on them as he was.

Farah threw herself forward again, unbothered by any water going up her nose in the race to reach him. He reached out his arms and took her hands but kept walking back, pulling her along with him. With every little kick of her feet she sent a shower of water up over Isolde, but she was just as excited as Amir to see her progress and wasn't fazed at all by being splashed.

'You're doing brilliantly, Farah, keep going,'

Isolde encouraged, keeping up pace alongside to make sure she was safe.

Amir could see for himself how much Isolde cared for his daughter, even if she was afraid to admit it. It was this commitment, this certainty that she wanted only the best for Farah too, that convinced him they should try and make things work as a couple, maybe even as a family. He would have to tread carefully, not frighten her off before they had a chance to be a couple, by putting the 'f' word out there. It was scary for him too, opening up their lives to include someone else when he and Farah were used to being a duo. Even though Isolde had been a part of their world for a while, making that transition from colleague and friend to something more was a big step for all of them.

In a way it had been easier when it was just the two of them. Apart from Farah's struggle to walk again, and the guilt and grief that had plagued him. But at least he hadn't had to answer to anyone else. He hadn't had to walk on eggshells, or moderate his behaviour or emotions through fear of upsetting a partner. All he'd had to do was focus on getting his daughter better. Now Farah was making progress he was beginning to look to the future. He didn't want to be on his own for ever, and though he hadn't wanted to be with someone who clearly thought he wasn't good enough, he knew Isolde wasn't that person.

When Farah grew tired he scooped her up and carried her back to the lounger. Isolde followed them out of the water and once more he was tormented by the sight of her in that barely there bikini, knowing he couldn't touch her until they were safe behind closed doors later tonight.

'Amir, can I have a word?' Isolde waited until he had Farah settled with her tablet and earphones watching her favourite video clips on the Internet.

It would give them a chance for a serious private conversation about the future without their raging libidos getting in the way. Thankfully she pulled her coverall back over her head, at least giving the illusion of wearing clothes that would hopefully prevent him being distracted so he could focus on the things he had to say to Isolde. The question he had to ask her.

She waited for him at the edge of the water and they walked a little together, far enough that Farah couldn't hear them, but where they could still keep an eye on her.

'I wanted to speak to you as well. I think we should—'

'This isn't going to work,' Isolde interrupted him.

'I know, it's obvious that we're together. Maybe we should try and cool things while we're out here but I thought once we're home we should try and make a go of it. As a couple,' he clarified.

Isolde blinked at him. 'You know I can't do that.'

'I know you're wary, especially with Farah involved, but I think it's worth taking the chance, don't you?' Amir rested his hands on her shoulders, desperately wanting to gather her into his arms and kiss her as he'd been able to this morning pre-breakfast. He'd be able to resist if he thought it was only a matter of time before they could be together all the time.

When Isolde shook her head he thought his heart had been ripped out of his chest.

'No. I told you I didn't want this. Farah's getting too attached and I, I can't promise either of you what you want, what you need. It wouldn't be fair on any of us. I have to go.' She walked away before he even had the chance to react, collecting her things from the lounger and putting her shoes back on.

'Now? Wait until we can get back to the palace and we can talk about this some more in private.' Of course she was going to have a wobble when it was everything she'd told him she was afraid of, getting involved with a single father, but he knew they had something good together. If only he could get her to look past her fears and concentrate on the present, they could have a chance.

'It's over, Amir. There's no point in living in dream land any more. I'll walk back to the palace.'

'You don't have to do that, Isolde. Don't put yourself in danger. Just get in the car. Please.'

He knew they'd put her under pressure to be a part of their day, and perhaps it had been too much to expect when she'd asked for space. Amir chastised himself for rushing her to a place she wasn't ready to go just yet. Hopefully there was still time to undo any damage before they went back to England. He didn't want to lose her now.

'No. I'll go on foot, thanks. I need the space.' Clutching her belongings, Isolde turned her back on him and started walking.

Amir had a horrible feeling it was the last

time he was going to see her again, but as much as he wanted to go after her, he couldn't leave Farah. He was torn, and that was the problem.

Isolde's heart was cracking right down the centre. It was painful and debilitating, and all her own fault. Despite knowing all the risks of getting involved with Amir, she'd pushed and pushed the boundaries until her emotions were well and truly unlocked. Now she had to suffer the pain of her heart breaking as a consequence.

She'd fallen for Amir, and Farah, wanted nothing more than to be part of their family, but she wasn't what they needed. He'd realise that soon enough. Better he did that now than when she'd damaged his relationship with his daughter beyond repair. At least she only had herself to worry about. Amir would have to find an explanation for Farah for her sudden retreat from their lives, but it was for her own good in the long run.

Today had brought all of her fears to life about getting involved with Amir. Not only had she realised how ingrained she was becoming into their lives, but the chance of disrupting their father/daughter relationship was very real. They were both coming to rely on a person who'd never taken responsibility for anything in her life. Even now she couldn't face her own emotions, knowing she cared very deeply for the pair, but walking away nonetheless. Proving the point to everyone involved that she was a bad bet.

Since Amir wasn't racing after her, or forcing the chauffeur to follow her journey, Isolde had to assume he'd come to that conclusion in the end too. He'd stayed with his daughter, and that was the right decision. Even if she felt lonelier than ever.

Warm salty tears streaked her face as she walked along the rough dirt track back towards the palace. Her discomfort as the stones penetrated the thin soles of her beach sandals felt like a just punishment for her stupidity but she needed the space from Amir and Farah to think clearly. Something she clearly hadn't been doing since the wedding. Their time together had been amazing, but a mistake. One she couldn't afford to repeat.

To avoid another lapse she was going to pack her bags and book the first flight out. Hopefully now Farah was making progress, Amir would be too caught up with his daughter to make a scene over her departure.

With Soraya and Raed on honeymoon too she could slip away without any fuss. Now the celebrations were over she was merely a guest in danger of outstaying her welcome anyway. A simple note of thanks to her generous hosts would have to suffice because she couldn't bear to say her goodbyes. They were more painful than she could ever have imagined.

CHAPTER NINE

'IT'S SO GOOD to hear your voice, Isolde. I still find it odd not speaking to you every day.' Soraya sighed on the other end of the phone.

'You were the one who went and got married,' she teased. 'We've both been busy but I'm sure we'll catch up with each other at some point.'

Isolde felt that familiar twinge of guilt and sadness she always got when reminded that she was very much on her own these days. Not only had she left Amir, Farah, and the rest of the family back there, but she'd handed in her notice at the hospital, doing her best to avoid the Ayads in her last weeks of work. Unable to face seeing them again, she'd got another physio to help with Farah and made sure she was working different shifts from Amir. She had thought a trip away touring Europe whilst she decided on her next step would give her the time and distance to get over her heartbreak. Yet it hadn't satisfied her the way she'd hoped. When she got back she planned starting afresh at a new job, meeting new people, but the closer her return date, the more she was dreading going back to a life without Amir, Farah and Soraya. A life without her family.

It had been a lovely trip but it hadn't solved anything. She'd expected to revel in her freedom, not having responsibilities to family or work. Being the Isolde she used to be. Walking around the Louvre in Paris and visiting chocolate shops in Belgium on her own hadn't been as much fun as she'd expected. It had only made her realise how much she was missing her loved ones.

'I…er…have something to tell you…' Soraya said ominously.

Isolde would've assumed she was about to announce a honeymoon baby was on the way, except her sister's hesitant tone suggested it wasn't good news she was about to impart.

'What is it? Is everything all right?' During her trip away, she'd kept contact to a minimum. Partly because she didn't want to be reminded of everything she'd left behind. Namely Amir. She hadn't heard a word about him, changing the subject any time Soraya mentioned him in a call, and had successfully avoided him at work by leaving. Hopefully one day she'd be back in the job she loved. She might even meet someone who'd make her forget Amir, but right now it didn't feel possible.

Soraya took a deep breath. 'Amir and Farah have moved back with us.'

Silence descended as Isolde processed that. Isolde only realised it had gone on too long when Soraya came on the line again. 'Isolde? Can you hear me? Are you there?'

Then she had to respond. Regardless of her world having just been upended all over again. 'Yes. I heard you.'

'He decided he wanted to have his family around him again. I guess to support him and Farah while she works on her mobility. What happened between you two anyway? You seemed so close to him and Farah at the wedding, then the next thing I heard you'd gone home without them.'

Isolde didn't like keeping secrets from her sister but she didn't want to make things any more awkward in the family. Especially if Amir was living over there now too. 'What has he said?'

'Nothing. He doesn't say much any more unless he's talking about Farah. It's as though the light has gone out of his eyes. Raed said he hasn't seen him like this since the accident. What happened, Isolde? I saw you together. I know something was going on.'

Even from this distance it seemed she couldn't keep anything from her big sister.

'One night, Soraya. That's all it was.'

'Oh, Isolde.' The sound of despair and disappointment in her sibling's voice made Isolde wince.

'He wanted more than I could give him,' she said quietly, the pain starting all over again.

'What were you thinking, Isolde? He and Farah have been through so much already.'

'Why do you think I ended it? They both need someone who can take on the responsibility of being a parent. We all know that's not me. I'm too selfish.'

Soraya tutted. 'That's nonsense. I've seen how you are with Farah, and Amir for that matter. I know it's scary making that sort of commitment. Believe me, I had a wobble before Raed and I finally got together, but it's worth taking the risk. If I thought you didn't love them I'd say fine, move on, enjoy your travels, but I can hear in your voice that you're not happy. Why else would you be phoning me when you're in one of the most romantic cities in the world?'

'For company…' Isolde looked up at the Eiffel Tower twinkling in the evening light and knew she'd do anything to see Farah's face, to be with Amir. In the back of her mind she'd chosen Paris thinking some handsome Frenchman might sweep her off her feet and kiss her until she forgot all about Amir. Except he was the only man she wanted kissing her.

She'd made a big mistake. Huge.

Her fear of causing the same sort of trauma she and Soraya had gone through as children had prevented her from committing to Amir, but she hadn't taken her own feelings into account. How much she missed him and Farah, or that she'd fallen in love with him. It was difficult to admit that to herself.

Perhaps that was even what she'd been running away from. If there was one thing that defined her move into the world of maturity it was acknowledging her feelings. She hadn't been ready when Amir had asked her to commit to more than a fling, but now not having him in her life at all seemed a worse fate. Quitting her job, flying off on a whim, doing all of those things that she associated with her younger, carefree self simply weren't that fun any more. The last time she'd had that was the day on the beach with Amir and Farah, watching her swim to her proud father. Before she'd freaked out about having actual feelings for someone and run away.

'So, do you want me to tell him you're on your way or…?'

Isolde hated that her sister knew her so well. Better than she even knew herself.

'Hey, Fa-Fa, you want to come with us to the centre today?' Raed came to join Amir and Farah in the garden.

Amir had taken her out for some fresh air after her morning's physio session. She was still in her wheelchair for most of the time but she was making progress. The only problem now was the transition from Isolde to the new physio. It wasn't that Sam wasn't good at his job. He was patient and enthusiastic. He just wasn't Isolde. Farah wasn't responding to him the way she did with Isolde and Amir couldn't blame her when he felt the same. No one could replace Isolde.

'Can I, Papa?'

'Well, I thought we were going to have lunch out here today, together?'

'We do that every day, Papa,' she said, rolling her eyes.

It would be an understatement to say that things hadn't worked out the way he'd planned. After Isolde had left he'd tried to carry on as normal, looking after Farah and working at the hospital when they'd returned to London. Except he'd just been going through the motions. Farah had been upset and confused, as he had been too when he'd discovered Isolde had left the hospital altogether. He'd messed things up for all of them.

Moving here was supposed to be a new start where they had family to support them and help them settle down. Farrah had started a new private school and made some friends, but he was finding it harder to adjust. Raed and Soraya had got him involved at the centre but he was missing the dynamic atmosphere of the hospital. More than that, he missed Isolde.

He'd left everything of her behind, but the memories of their time together burned brightly still in his mind. According to Soraya she was travelling, currently in Paris, living her best life. It felt as though she was trying to prove to him how unsuitable she was as a long-term partner by quitting her job and taking off on a whim, but he wasn't quite buying it. He knew how much she loved her job, and Farah. There was even a sneaking suspicion that she had feelings for him that went beyond the bedroom, and that was why she'd got on the first flight home as soon as he'd suggested moving their relationship to something more serious.

Soraya had hinted at the same, though she hadn't elaborated. He knew they'd been in contact recently but all she'd said was that she didn't believe her sister was happy. It didn't do anything to make him feel better. He hadn't chased her back to London, or even sought her out when he had returned, because he'd thought that was what she wanted. If she wasn't any happier he wondered if the sacrifice had been worth it. They could've had something special but they'd thrown it away in the attempt to prevent each other from being hurt, to make them happy. Well, he was hurt and he certainly wasn't happy.

'Maybe I could come with you? I'm sure there's something I can find to keep me busy.' If Fahid wasn't there for him to check in with, he was sure there was something to keep him busier there than here. The gardener wasn't keen on him 'helping' with the pruning, weeding, or anything else he'd tried to do to keep his mind off Isolde and who she might be with in Paris. He didn't want to think of her walking arm in arm along the Champs-Élysées with a handsome stranger, stopping for dinner and a bottle of wine in some quaint bistro… Yeah, he'd been thinking about that way too much.

'Er… I think you'd be better staying here. There's a delivery coming today,' Soraya told him as she arrived on the scene.

'Can't the staff take it in?' He didn't understand why she was using such a lame excuse to get rid of him when they all knew collecting the mail was not something the royal family dirtied their hands with when living at the palace.

'No…er…this is one you're going to want to be here for yourself.' Apparently it was Raed's turn to fob him off. Amir didn't miss the shifty look he shot Soraya. Something was going on and they clearly didn't want him at the centre.

'Fine. Go do your secret stuff and I'll wait here.' He threw his hands up, not wanting to stand in the way if they'd planned something special with Farah today. They were very good at including her in things. That at least justified his reasons for uprooting them to come out here.

'Yeah, we need to leave. Amir, no offence but you might want to have a shave and change your clothes, bro.' Raed checked his watch and made a gesture to Soraya that Amir wasn't sure he was supposed to have seen.

'It's that special a delivery, huh?' he asked no one in particular as the troublesome trio were already hightailing it out of the gardens.

A glimpse of himself in the windows of the summer house told him perhaps his brother was right. He was beginning to look as bad as he felt.

Isolde's arrival into the country was an altogether different experience when she wasn't travelling as part of the royal family. Soraya and Raed had wanted to pull out all the stops for her but that kind of went against the idea of her low-key visit. She didn't want fanfares and golden carriages heralding her arrival in case Amir didn't want her. In which case she'd be leaving with her tail firmly between her legs and her dignity trailing on the ground behind her.

However, the crowded economy seats on the plane, the overly hot, bumpy bus journey and the racing driver currently masquerading as her taxi transfer were making her rethink returning to her civilian status here so quickly.

Turning up at the palace gates completely unannounced would not have guaranteed her entry, so Soraya and Raed had made arrangements ahead of her arrival. It didn't make the security any less intimidating on the way in.

She wanted to slip in to shower and change after her journey, before she went to find Amir. Soraya had texted to say they'd taken Farah out for the day. Though she was sorry not to see her again, Isolde was glad she and Amir would hopefully have privacy to talk. Despite her sister's assurance that he was missing her, she couldn't be one hundred per cent certain he'd be happy to see her, never mind want to pick up where they'd left off. It had been a big step for him to invite her into his life, and Farah's, and she'd thrown it back in his face. There was no way of knowing if he'd forgive her for that, or indeed, with some time and distance, realise he'd had a lucky escape.

Now it was her turn to show her hand, to

tell him she'd made a mistake, and that she loved him, wanted him back. Then it was down to Amir to decide if there was any chance of a future together. If he said no she was on a plane back to England. There was no way she could stay if he didn't want her. In fact any family get-togethers were going to be off limits because she couldn't stand the humiliation and heartache of seeing him, perhaps even with a new partner.

The thought alone made her queasy. It was becoming clear to her she was only here because of her assumption he still wanted her in his life. If she'd missed her chance to be with him, she didn't think she'd ever recover from it.

Instead of heading into the palace she found herself veering off into the gardens for some fresh air to stop her head spinning, and somewhere to sit before her legs gave way.

'Isolde? What are you doing here?' Amir appeared before her, the sun shining behind his head to give him an ethereal look that made her wonder if she'd conjured him up in her imagination.

Then he took her hand in his and she knew he was real. 'Are you okay? You don't look well.'

'This wasn't how it was supposed to be...'
She hadn't meant to say it aloud, but this was
all wrong. In all the plans she'd made, all
the scenarios she'd dreamed, she looked so
ravishing he couldn't resist. Not so tired and
dishevelled he thought she needed an ambulance.

'What's happened, Isolde? I thought you
were in Paris?' He sat down beside her, still
clutching her hand, but Isolde figured that
was out of concern rather than his desperate
need to touch her again.

'I was. I left. I came back.'

'So I see.' His smile was as beautiful as
she remembered and she wondered how
she'd ever found the strength to leave him,
and why.

'I had some time to think, and I, I wanted
to see you again.' She was struggling to
find the words she knew she needed to say
to make this journey worth it, but she was
afraid they weren't enough to get the result
she wanted.

'Oh? Are you the special delivery I'm supposed to be waiting for?' he asked with a
smirk. At least he didn't seem disappointed
or angry with her. It was a start.

'I guess so. I'm sorry how we left things.

How I left things.' It was entirely her fault and she accepted that.

He was frowning now, the memory of the last time they'd seen each other clearly not a happy one for either of them. 'By the time we came back to the palace that day you'd already gone. Farah was so upset. As was I.'

Hearing it didn't make what she had to say any easier. Okay, so he'd wanted her to stay, but she hadn't, and it was bound to have affected how he felt about her. Especially when she'd caused distress to his daughter too by leaving without another word.

'I'm sorry. I handled things badly. But I was afraid if I stayed you'd change my mind.'

At that, Amir stopped scowling, his eyes wide with surprise at the knowledge that he'd had the power to make her stay all along. 'You seemed so dead set on leaving. I didn't think you wanted to be with us. With me.'

His words reached in and squeezed Isolde's heart. Knowing she'd hurt him enough to feel that way was devastating.

'It was all I wanted but I thought I was being selfish. That you needed a real grown-up.' She smiled at that. If her time away had taught her anything it was that she was an adult with real, grown-up emotions that couldn't be silenced by last-minute holidays drinking wine on her own.

'And now?'

Isolde swallowed the anxiety creeping up and threatening to overwhelm her with thoughts that this wasn't the right thing to do, that opening up her heart to him was only going to cause more heartache for both of them. But what choice did she have? If she went home now without even trying, she would be back at square one, unsettled, unhappy, and uncertain that she'd done the right thing.

She took a deep breath. 'I've had feelings for you for a long time, Amir. That night together…it awakened something stronger that frightened me. I'm no use at long-term relationships, and I can't guarantee I'll make a good partner to you, or role model for Farah. I don't want to hurt either of you. I never did. But I thought I should at least tell you how I feel.'

'You haven't put a name to it yet. I mean, I understand you're frightened about getting into something serious. So am I. The only way we'll hurt each other is by keeping things to ourselves. We need to be honest, and that includes how we feel about one another. I moved out here with Farah because I couldn't bear life back in London without you. So, in case you're in any doubt, Isolde Yarrow, I'm in love with you.'

A choir of angels sang out her relief as he put her out of her misery by saying the words first so she knew she was safe to say them too. 'I love you too, Amir. I was just afraid to admit it, even to myself.'

The moment the words left her lips he caught them in a kiss. Her sigh of contentment filled the air.

Being with Amir again, feeling that security of his arms around her, was everything she'd been searching for. She just hadn't realised it.

EPILOGUE

'THIS IS THE LIFE.' Isolde lay back on the lounger and let the sun warm her face.

'We need to make the most of the peace and quiet,' Amir said as he lay down beside her.

Isolde instinctively put a hand on her swollen belly, thinking about the chaos that would descend in just a couple of months' time. A baby hadn't been on their agenda at all, but theirs had been conceived on the night of the wedding at the palace.

Although she'd never expected to be a mother, finding out she was expecting Amir's baby had made her feel complete. She had Amir, Farah, her sister, and the rest of the royal family around her, but finally she knew she'd found her role. The idea of being a parent had always terrified her—she'd thought she would screw it up as badly as her parents had—but being around Farah had shown her she was capable of taking on that responsibility and love for a child. Isolde was lucky Amir and Farah had come into her life. She'd never known such love.

'Farah is going to make a wonderful big sister.' The little girl was working so hard to get back on her feet so she'd be able to play with her new brother or sister it was heartwarming. She'd been over the moon when Isolde and Amir had officially become a couple, and hearing there was a baby on the way had made her cry as many happy tears as her father when he'd found out.

'And cousin. There are big changes coming.' Amir grinned.

Not long after her positive pregnancy test, Soraya had announced she and Raed were having a honeymoon baby too. All working together at the centre and living together at the palace had finally given her a true sense of family. Everything was going so well for them both she was afraid to believe it was real.

She reached out a hand to take Amir's. 'Thank you. I can't remember ever being this happy.'

He smiled at her and her heart grew two

sizes. She loved him so much she couldn't believe she'd ever been afraid to acknowledge it.

Amir swung his legs around so he was sitting on the edge of his sunbed and rummaged in the bag they'd brought with them to the beach.

'What are you looking for?' she asked, sitting up to see if she could help, but he didn't answer.

Instead he got up off the lounger and knelt in the sand between their two beds.

'What are you doing? You'll burn yourself on the sand.'

Amir held out a small box and opened it to reveal a diamond and platinum ring sparkling so much in the sun it nearly blinded Isolde. 'This is the happiest I've ever been too, but I want to make things official. Isolde Yarrow, would you do me the honour of being my wife?'

She could see the uncertainty on his face and understood his reservations about asking her when she'd protested against any sort of commitment for so long. But affirming their love for one another in a ceremony made him hers as much as the other way around and she didn't want to be without him ever again.

'Yes. There's nothing I'd love more than

to be your wife, Amir.' Isolde held her hand out and watched as he slipped the ring on her finger before pulling her into an embrace.

Their family was getting bigger by the day and she couldn't be happier about it.

* * * * *

If you missed the previous story in the Royal Docs duet, then check out

Surgeon Prince's Fake Fiancée

And if you enjoyed this story, check out these other great reads from Karin Baine

Nurse's Risk with the Rebel
Falling Again for the Surgeon
Single Dad for the Heart Doctor

All available now!